"This is your basic baptism by fire,"

Catherine commented with a grin. "If you can make it through a day with three active kids, being presented with them one at a time ought to be a piece of cake."

Jay studied her. Wisps of fine brown hair framed her face, her eyes were lit with the gentle glow of a burning candle, her cheeks were flushed and healthy looking.

"You're not a Catherine," he stated while tentatively touching a lightly freckled, slightly sunburned cheek. "Nor a Catherine Rose. There's too much life and vibrancy in you for such prim and proper names. You're a Rosie," he informed her positively. "With a red rose's vibrant hues and its deceiving surface fragility, but mostly its flair and capacity for transmitting pleasure to its beholder...."

Dear Reader,

When I think of the month of June, I summon up images of warm spring days with the promise of summer, joyous weddings and, of course, the romance that gets the man of your dreams to the point where he can celebrate Father's Day.

And that's what June 1990 is all about here at Silhouette Romance. Our DIAMOND JUBILEE is in full swing, and this month features *Cimarron Knight*, by Pepper Adams—the first book in Pepper's *Cimarron Stories* trilogy. Hero Brody Sawyer gets the shock of his life when he meets up with delightful Noelle Chandler. Then in July, don't miss *Borrowed Baby*, by Marie Ferrarella. Brooding loner Griffin Foster is in for a surprise when he finds that his sister has left him with a little bundle of joy!

The DIAMOND JUBILEE—Silhouette Romance's tenth anniversary celebration—is our way of saying thanks to you, our readers. To symbolize the timelessness of love, as well as the modern gift of the tenth anniversary, we're presenting readers with a DIAMOND JUBILEE Silhouette Romance title each month, penned by one of your favorite Silhouette Romance authors. In the coming months, many of your favorite writers, including Lucy Gordon, Dixie Browning, Phyllis Halldorson and Annette Broadrick, are writing DIAMOND JUBILEE titles especially for you.

And that's not all! There are six books a month from Silhouette Romance—stories by wonderful authors who time and time again bring home the magic of love. During our jubilee year, each book is special and written with romance in mind. June brings you *Fearless Father*, by Terry Essig, as well as *A Season for Homecoming*, the first book in Laurie Paige's duo, *Homeward Bound*. And much-loved Diana Palmer has some special treats in store in the months ahead.

I hope you'll enjoy this book and all the stories to come. Come home to romance—Silhouette Romance—for always!

Sincerely,

Tara Hughes Gavin
Senior Editor

TERRY ESSIG

Fearless Father

Silhouette Romance

Published by Silhouette Books New York

America's Publisher of Contemporary Romance

For J. D. Parent
Dad, you always told me I could be and do
whatever I wanted.
Why didn't I believe you?

SILHOUETTE BOOKS
300 E. 42nd St., New York, N.Y. 10017

ISBN: 0-373-08725-X

First Silhouette Books printing June 1990

Printed in the U.S.A.

Books by Terry Essig

Silhouette Romance

House Calls #552
The Wedding March #662
Fearless Father #725

TERRY ESSIG

says that her writing is her escape from a life that leaves very little time for recreation or hobbies. With a husband and six young children, Terry works on her stories a little at a time, between seeing to her children's piano, sax and trombone lessons, their gymnastics, ice-skating and swim-team practices, and her own activities of leading a brownie troop, participating in a car pool and attending organic chemistry classes. Her ideas, she says, come from her imagination and her life—neither one of which is lacking!

Chapter One

Futilitarian. Pessimist seeing no particular point to anything in life.

Catherine Rose Escabito carefully peeled the narrow strip of sticky tape holding the ochre vocabulary card to the lower left corner of the bathroom's metal medicine cabinet. Studying it one last time, she crumpled it into a tight ball and deposited word ten in this month's self-improvement plan neatly into the white plastic wastebasket that sat next to the sink.

No matter how hard she had tried the previous day, she had simply been unable to casually work the word into her conversation. Everything she had thought of had sounded stilted and awkward.

Sighing, Catherine reached into the medicine cabinet for the roll of tape. She pulled a four-inch length free only to have it turn back on itself and stick together. Knowing better than to try straightening out the convoluted mess, she wadded it up, tossed it into the wastebasket with yesterday's word of the day and started over. She stuck a new piece of tape onto the edge of the sink as she reached into the box for the next card. Maybe today's word would be a little more manageable.

Her eyes closed in resignation as she viewed the new card. *Mulct.* Who in the devil had stayed up late at night digging that one up? *Ninety Days to a Richer Vocabulary* would make a futilitarian of her yet. She perked up at that. Not bad. There was hope. Squinting—she did *not* need glasses— she went back to read the new word's definition. *Deprive of a possession unjustly.* Hmm. If only she could lead a conversation into a discussion on the IRS. She *still* felt she'd been in the right three years ago when—but there was no past tense given. Was it like burst, the same in present and past? Had the IRS *mulct* her or *mulcted* her three years ago?

Catherine pondered the past tense of mulct as she leaned over the sink's slightly discolored porcelain bowl and taped up the new card. Oh, well, she had all day to come up with something.

She turned on the taps and splashed water on her face. It would be convenient if a con artist would show up at the grocery store where she worked this afternoon and try to swindle—or perhaps mulct—the place. Naturally she'd be onto him before he got away with anything and have a terrific opportunity to use a new word. She patted her face dry with one of her new plush terry hand towels and reveled in its soft caress, so different from the scratchy old ones they'd replaced the day before. Heaven right here on earth.

On her way back to the bedroom in quest of shorts and a top, she froze in the hallway. Someone was pounding on her back door. Who could it possibly be? She stood there in her shorty pajamas and robe while she considered the possibilities. There weren't many.

The apartment complex was set up so that Catherine's front entrance foyer and steps up to her third-floor apartment were shared with her eastern neighbor, a widower recently retired from the park district's maintenance corps. He never bothered her, preferring the company of his three cats. Besides, he'd have used the front door. It was all they shared.

The rear landing and wooden stair egress was also communal, but with the neighbor to the west. Iris would often knock on the back kitchen door to borrow some forgotten spice or condiment. She doubted it was Iris though, as Catherine knew she hadn't mentioned to her friend that she'd switched shifts with Beth Anne, the grocery store's night clerk, to accommodate one of Beth Anne's heavy dates. Therefore, Iris would assume Catherine was at work at this time of day. The only other possibility was the building super. And that man was decidedly strange. Catherine wasn't up to facing him in pink and white candy-striped baby dolls and a shorty robe. He made her nervous enough when she faced him fully dressed. She wouldn't let him in. There was nothing broken or backed up that she knew about in the apartment.

A second impatient knock told her there would be no time to quickly change. So she clutched her robe tightly together at her neck—as though that would make up for its minimal length—and made her way toward the kitchen.

Hiding behind the dining room wall, she poked just her head around the kitchen door opening. The four-paned window in her kitchen door gave a rather frightening view of the chest, neck, and chin of a man so tall that the top of the door cut the view off midnose. Make no mistake, the guy was *large*. Also a total stranger. She'd never seen that broad chest, strong chin or half nose before. What was this imposing specimen doing at her back door?

"Yes?" she called from her spot behind the door. "What do you want?"

Catherine watched as the man turned from a profile view to stoop and peer through the door's glass panes. She really would have to think about hanging some kind of privacy curtain. The thing was, she'd always thought herself safe enough from peepers up here on the third floor. Now she knew better.

"Hello? I'm trying to find . . ." Catherine couldn't catch what it was he was trying to find. The barrier of the door and the distance from her position in the dining room was too great. "Hello?" he called again.

"I'm sorry, I can't understand you. What did you say?" she called, more wary than ever. A person would have to be strange indeed to climb to a third-floor apartment for directions when there was a gas station on the corner. What if he was casing the building, looking for an empty apartment to rob? She probably ought to phone the police.

"What?" the man called, cupping a hand to his ear. "I can't hear you."

Darn. She was going to have to get closer to the door if she was ever going to understand enough to send him on his way. Catherine looked down at the cloud of pink and white nylon swirling provocatively at the top of her thighs. She guessed she looked all of twelve instead of her own twenty-four. She was wrong.

"Well, at least I haven't unlocked the door yet to catch the morning breeze," she muttered under her breath as she swung from behind the doorframe and walked through the kitchen to the door with assumed nonchalance. As she reached the rear door she noticed the man's squint open into wide-eyed astonishment as he took in her attire. His eyes were a warm brown that matched his casually waving hair with uncanny accuracy. It was an unusual combination.

Effective. Worthy of a second and, yes, even a third glance. She grew warm when she saw the way his gaze slid down the length of his strong nose and onto her. He was studying the way her pink and white baby dolls clung and delineated the contours of her breasts.

She grew impatient as the perusal became more assessing. Forcing her hands to release their death grip on the neck of her robe, she allowed it to fall a little more loosely and naturally around her body. "What do you want?" she inquired in as icy a manner as she could muster.

The man's eyes snapped back up to her face. He muttered something she couldn't quite make out before speaking more loudly. "I'm looking for my brother, Hollis Gand. I believe this is their apartment next to yours? Do you know where they might be?"

With a frown, Catherine thought back. Iris had never mentioned a brother-in-law to her. And in the middle of a weekday morning, where did he think Hollis was? "Why aren't you using the front entrance instead of sneaking up the rear?" she questioned suspiciously.

"I did," the man protested self-righteously, obviously not used to being questioned. "I thought the buzzer might be broken when nobody responded, so I tried the back, but I don't think anybody's home. I can't understand it. I wrote two weeks ago to say I was coming, and after a six-hour drive from southern Illinois, I'm beat." He took a slightly crumpled white handkerchief from somewhere below her view and wiped his face while commenting distractedly, "It's getting hotter than the hinges of Hades out here. I hope they're not planning on being away long. Baking in that hot metal car another hour or two is not my idea of a good time."

Then again, Iris had rarely mentioned her husband's family at all in the six months Catherine had known her.

Their conversations had jumped with the discontinuity Catherine was finding typical of Iris. The woman went from one lively topic to the next but had yet to touch much on family or roots—other than her horrid mother-in-law. "Look, I'm really sorry. But I don't know where Iris is. I assume Hollis is at work, and Iris could be anywhere. She likes to take the kids to the park or beach mornings so they'll be tired and take a long nap. I don't know what to tell you. Are you sure they got the letter?"

The man let loose an exasperated sigh from between pursed lips. "No, I'm not sure. I didn't think to double check. Could you please open the door? It's really difficult to talk this way. And I'd be eternally in your debt if you'd give me a glass of water and let me use your bathroom." His right eye began to wink.

Catherine took in the blinking eye with a touch of asperity. Men could be *so* obvious. Did he really think such a blatant gesture would move her to let a total stranger into the apartment with her? "How do I know you're Hollis's brother? And kindly stop winking at me. That's not going to get you anyplace."

The man flushed and turned sideways again. "Sorry," he murmured. Routing through a pocket, he eventually held up a rather mangled brown leather wallet, which he flipped open and held up to the windowpane. Through the distortion of the glass and the wallet's blurry cellophane card holder, Catherine could just make out the details of a California driver's license in the name of one Julius John Gand, six foot four, one hundred and ninety-five pounds, born on the twelfth of June. Jeepers, Julius John? Well, it fit right in with Hollis George. She reached for the skeleton key she had left sticking out of the door's lock and gave it a twist while turning the doorknob in the opposite direction and kicking the bottom panel with a well-aimed blow of her toes. The door had a tendency to stick in humid weather.

Successfully opening the heavy inner wooden door, she pushed the screen door in the opposite direction and invited Julius Gand inside. "Come in, Mr. Gand. You may certainly use the bathroom. I just hope you haven't made a six-hour drive for nothing. I'll get dressed and make some orange juice."

He sidled past her, keeping the right side of his face averted as he went. "A glass of water will be fine, ma'am. I don't want to put you to any trouble. I just didn't want to sit in that car for another second."

"No problem," she dismissed airily, fully convinced now that he was who he said. Without the door obscuring her view, she could see that the short-sleeved pale blue broadcloth shirt he wore had to be admired for the subtle way it clung to the muscled breadth of his torso. Soft now after many washings, it was neatly tucked into loose-fitting navy cotton duck pants. His feet were encased in supple leather docksiders, their color a close match to his impossibly thick hair and warm eyes. The breeze stirred by his passage held a hint of men's cologne, and Catherine sniffed the air in appreciation. "I was going to make myself some breakfast as soon as I'd dressed. If you haven't eaten, I'd be happy to throw on an extra egg or two."

He passed a weary hand over his eyes and smiled tiredly. "If you're sure it's not a problem, I'd be delighted. I had planned the trip to get here in time for breakfast with Iris and the kids, but I guess that's not going to happen."

Catherine guessed not. He didn't know much about children if he thought breakfast would just be getting under way at nine in the morning. Iris's three kids were up with the sun. Breakfast was nothing but a fond memory by this time of day.

He shrugged his shoulders in a gesture of defeat. Mercy, his shoulders were broad! Catherine cleared her throat. "Uh, hum. Well, I'll just get dressed. The bathroom is this way." She passed by him and led the way back through the dining room, living room, and down the narrow front hallway. He smiled vaguely in her direction and she had to concentrate on not stuttering as she organized things. "The towels are fresh, I just put them out. I'll meet you back in the kitchen when you're ready." She left him at the bath's entrance to enter her own room, closing the door tightly behind her and taking a deep breath to still the strange flutters in her stomach.

He was already in the kitchen when she returned. "You know, Julius," she began conversationally. "You probably should have called to make sure Hollis and Iris got your note. We've become fairly good friends since I moved in six months ago, and I'm sure she would have mentioned an impending in-law visit."

"It's not quite as bad as the plague, I assure you. One would hope they don't see me as a blight on their horizon to discuss with the neighbors." He laughed a little, sending a shiver of pleasure down Catherine's spine. "Anyway, please call me Jay, blight or not."

Catherine could understand that. It was certainly preferable to Julius or Juli. What had the woman who bore him been thinking of? "Julius is a rather unusual name," she offered tentatively before reverting to safer matters. "How many eggs?"

"Julius is a family name, and not as uncommon as you might think. Remember Julius Irving, Dr. J.? Great basketball player." He viewed the sliced onion and chopped pepper sautéing in the frying pan with interest and noted the growing pile of grated cheese. "Four. I love omelets."

Four? A growing boy, evidently.

She paused in the act of cracking an egg, momentarily disconcerted. "I'm sorry, but I've never been able to successfully fold an omelet. I gave up trying. These are going to be scrambled." Why was she apologizing? Hadn't she promised herself to never apologize for what she was ever again? She was giving the guy breakfast, wasn't she? "If that's not all right, I can give you a pan so that you can do your own thing." If she sounded a bit defensive, he didn't seem to notice.

"What? Oh, good Lord, no. Scrambled is better than anything I could do." He paused, then confided, "Day-to-day practicalities like cooking tend to get away from me. I finally had to hire a housekeeper so I wouldn't starve to death." He shook his head. "Like checking with Iris. You'd think I'd have had the sense to pick up a phone and double-check things." Again he shook his head disparagingly. "But I'm afraid I'll have to admit the thought never entered my mind until you suggested it just now."

Catherine smiled into the bowl of five eggs while the delicious aroma of sautéed onions permeated the air. "That reminds me of my parents. Geniuses in their own right, but more than a tad flaky when it comes to the nitty-gritty."

"Oh, yeah? Should I recognize your last name?" Jay folded his large frame sideways into a cane Breuer's chair and looked up interestedly from his place at the small butcher-block table.

"Depends on your field, I guess. Dad is first violinist for the Chicago symphony and Mom's a chemical engineer. She's an energy expert and spends a lot of time in Washington trying to explain the facts of life to various congressional subcommittees. Martha Escabito. Ever hear of her?"

Jay thought about it. "Um, no. I don't think I ever have. Escabito. But I think I saw your dad last year when the symphony toured the west coast. Twice actually. Once in

L.A. and again in San Francisco. I don't know much about music, but I enjoy listening. Absolutely beautiful.''

Catherine poured the beaten eggs over the now tender onion and peppers, adding a handful of grated cheddar. She looked up from her position at the stove to study his handsomely chiseled profile. She was surprised by how little the disruption to her planned quiet morning at home bothered her. "What is it that you do know, Jay Gand?''

"Me? I'm a seismologist. Where do you keep the silverware? I can at least set the table.'' He jumped to his feet, almost taking out the low-hanging light fixture in the process.

Catherine used her stirring spoon to point out a drawer. "Over there. The plates are in the cupboard right above the silverware drawer.'' Then more to herself, she muttered reflectively, "A seismologist. That explains the California license." Probably gets his kicks camping out on top of the San Andreas fault.

The muscles of his arms and shoulders moved in lithe symmetry as Jay employed himself in the mundane task of counting out forks, knives, and spoons. He either hadn't noticed or had chosen to ignore her ruminations and she was taken by surprise when he turned and caught her staring. "What about you, Miss Escabito? What's your field of genius? Do you take after your father or your mother?''

"Call me Catherine,'' she directed and grimaced slightly. It did get tiring to constantly explain your own lack of brilliance in a star-studded family. "And I'm afraid my little brother and sister cornered the genetic brain pool. My parents were just practising when they had me. I inherited enough from both sides to make me nicely competent in many different areas, but I don't excel anywhere along the line.''

From the corner of his warm gaze, Jay studied her slim figure as she frowned at the texture of the thickening eggs. He watched her adjust the flame and noticed the way her cotton shorts pulled enticingly across her gently rounded rump as she leaned to make the adjustment. Her shirt gaped away from her breasts to show a tantalizing glimpse of gleaming cleavage and he could think of at least a few areas in which she excelled. And there was nothing wrong with the way her mint-green outfit set off the hidden fiery depths in her deep brown hair or the way her thick black lashes framed her widely spaced blue eyes. He turned to set the plates and mugs on the table and inquired in a level voice, "So, which area of mild competence have you chosen to pursue, Catherine? What do you do?"

It was silent for a moment as Catherine tried to judge his coming reaction. She'd just as soon avoid another lecture. But then, he couldn't know what her family thought about her job. "I'm head clerk at one of the Vincent's Better Foods. It's a small chain of groceries here in the area, if you're not familiar with the name." She turned to spoon the eggs onto their plates and sat down after placing the pan in the sink to soak.

Jay looked puzzled. Whether his expression was due to her career choice, or the closed, defensive look she knew she now wore was unclear. "You clerk in a grocery store?"

She guessed he didn't number many grocery checkers among his acquaintances. Next, she figured, he'd be trying to understand why anyone, especially someone with her genes, would want to do what she did.

"You decided to cop out of the family competition, is that it?"

So predictable. She could almost feel herself closing up. "I suppose a lesser informed type might go for a facile interpretation like that. The fact of the matter is, I enjoy

what I do." She made a deprecatory little gesture. "Oh, I
know, my degree in business is going to waste. I could be out
there sweating my way up the ladder of a company whose
product I don't give a fig about. But what would it get me
other than ulcers, late hours and nightmares over impending deadlines? This way, I get good pay for working clearly
defined hours. I've got time for myself and I've only had
two nightmares in the six years I've been there. Those were
back when I was actually checking groceries. Two women
within a week of each other insisted those horrid little hand-
held red clicker things were more accurate than my zillion-
dollar cash register and demanded a recheck of an entire
basketful of groceries. That kind of thing can get under your
skin. Generally, though, I'm free to pursue my evenings
without stewing about work. My job, being basically rote,
doesn't take a lot of mental gymnastics. My mind is my own
when I leave for the day. Not a bad arrangement, when you
stop to consider it."

She stopped to take a mouthful of eggs, savoring their
creamy texture and flavor before looking up. "Want some
toast? Are you so tall that your legs won't fit under the table? It must be uncomfortable eating sideways like that."

Catherine enjoyed much of life with an infectious enthu-
siasm. When she ate, every taste bud was called upon to
revel in the food presented, and she wanted those around her
equally content.

Jay looked decidedly awkward. In fact a dull red flush
crept up his neck as he sat crosswise in the chair, his breakfast plate held in one hand over his lap while the other hand
manipulated the fork. He shot her an embarrassed look before quickly averting his head again. "You didn't want me
winking at you," he muttered, nonplussed at the way Catherine had called him on the idiosyncrasy others made a
conscious effort to avoid. She was direct, if nothing.

"I think I must have missed something. What does your winking half an hour ago have to do with your sitting sideways to the table now?"

Jay spoke into his plate. "I wasn't winking half an hour ago. It's a muscle tick I can't control. The spasms are worse when I'm tired or upset. Right now I'm both, and since it seemed to be bothering you, I was trying to spare you."

Genuinely mortified, Catherine sputtered into her cup of orange juice before looking up. "Oh, my gosh, I'm sorry. I didn't know it was a physical thing. You have to understand, I thought you were winking at me so I'd let you in, and I hate men who know they're handsome and use blatant come-ons as if I hadn't any resistance to their magnetic sex appeal—I'm making it all worse, aren't I?"

Catherine's delicate peach-tinted skin tones were rapidly acquiring the same fiery tones Jay was displaying. "Listen, it's okay. I wasn't trying to make you feel bad. I'm used to it now."

Jay hated having to explain. He'd learned to live with it, but explanations always seemed to embarrass the other party. It had made him relatively shy and now he rarely ventured out into the field, preferring to work with the figures others brought back to him in his quiet lab. He'd only accepted this field opportunity because it presented a chance to spend some time with his brother. He'd been sadly remiss in that area in the past few years. Lord, little Emily must be five or six by now, and he had only seen her a handful of times. His godson, John, had recently turned four. Four-year-old speech was garbled enough without the additional translation problems caused by hundreds of miles of telephone lines. And there was a new little one. What . . . Tod, that was it. Must be closing in on a year by now.

So he'd left his self-imposed cloister, and now wished he hadn't for he knew he was making a spectacle of himself.

She was only being kind with her talk of thinking it part of his sex appeal. But he had reckoned without Catherine Rose Escabito herself. She was too used to feeling odd man out in her own family to ever knowingly let a guest in her home feel ill at ease. Now that she was over the initial surprise, she accepted the slight aberration and was determined to treat it as inconsequential. Like crooked teeth, of which hers were charmingly askew, or freckles, of which she had more than she considered her fair share peppered across the bridge of her straight nose. It was a physical fact having nothing to do with a person's inner beauty....

In a no-nonsense tone, Catherine straightforwardly directed, "Well, if that's all that's causing you to scrunch over your food like that, forget it. Turn around and put your plate on the table so you can enjoy it. I won't faint or anything if you blink a few times."

And she proceeded to direct the conversation along more innocuous lines while they listened with half an ear for Iris's return.

Finally, when the dishes were washed and the counters wiped with a sponge, Catherine realized she was going to have to get on with her day unless she wanted to go to work with nothing accomplished. She crooked her head to one side and looked the long distance up to his tanned features, considering them critically. "Of course, I don't know how fast your eye goes normally, but if it's true that it speeds up when you're tired and anxious, you must be exhausted. It's going hell-bent for leather. The problem is, Iris keeps talking about giving me a key to her apartment in case one of the kids locks her out, but she hasn't done it yet. You ought to lie down here and take a nap while you're waiting. You must have gotten up around two in the morning to have driven six hours by nine. Sleep for a while and by the time you wake up, I'm sure she'll be back. She's got to give the kids lunch and naps sooner or later. I'm going to lay carpeting in the bathroom, which should be relatively quiet unless I get to swearing. I promise you won't be in the way. Go ahead.'' It was all said while she effectively ushered the man twice her size down the hall and into her daintily feminine bedroom, leaving Jay to wonder at the manipulative capabilities of a slip of a woman a good six stone lighter than he.

Jay didn't recognize the Laura Ashley tiny print floral bedspread, but he eyed its pale blue tones dubiously.

''So fold it back, and don't get it dirty,'' Catherine directed him.

Ignoring that, his vision took in the bed's flounced apricot skirt, the window's apricot and blue tie-backs, sheered carefully on a brass rod, and the white wicker rocker's combination plain apricot and Ashley-print blue-ruffled pillows. The rocker was next to a small table hidden under a tiered floor-length skirt. It was a very feminine room. The proverbial bull in the china shop had nothing on him at the moment.

He took his shoes off just inside the doorway and his feet sank into the blue carpeting. Catherine was looking around her, a satisfied little smile on her face. ''This is the first room I finished,'' she confided. ''What do you think?''

''This carpeting is such a light color, aren't you concerned?'' he rasped, thoroughly off balance as the faint smell of recently spritzed perfume assaulted his senses.

Catherine answered hesitantly, as if reliving her decision-making. ''I thought about it, but there's only me, and so long as I take my shoes off and pull the ex-lite shade in the afternoon—blue fades terribly in direct light, you know—I should be all right. And I do love the look.''

''It's very, uh, dainty.''

Catherine looked pleased. "Yes, it is, isn't it? I'm glad it comes across. Sometimes you get too close to a project, you know? It takes an outsider to give you the final word. I was thinking of a silk floral arrangement in apricot and blue toward the end of the dresser." She indicated the side nearest the windows with an energetic gesture. "What do you think? Too much of a good thing?"

"Well, actually, I'm not much good at this kind of thing." He spread his hands in a helpless gesture. "As I think I already said, seismology is my—"

Catherine raised a finger knowingly, cutting off the rest of his remarks. "Right, I remember. Good in your field, but the mechanics of everyday living get away from you." She shrugged philosophically. "Oh, well, don't let it get you down. It's a nasty habit of mine, anyway. I ask all my friends' advice and then turn around and do the opposite. It's one of those things I can't seem to help. Makes for all kinds of ruffled feelings on the adviser's part. Since you haven't given an opinion, your feelings won't be hurt when I do whatever I want to do in the first place, will they?" She grinned, looking very pleased with her convoluted logic.

Jay had an odd sort of dazed expression on his face as he bent over and moved his shoes closer to the end of the bed and out of the traffic pattern of the doorway. He reached into his back pant's pocket and removed his keys and loose change, setting them on the small table next to the wicker rocker as she more or less bounced her way over to the dresser.

"I'll just take this roll of brown paper and my scissors and be out of your way."

"I thought you were going to put a rug in the bathroom."

"You have to make a pattern out of brown paper first. That way you can tape and patch until you've got it right and there'll be no major mistakes when you cut out the real rug."

Jay was sitting on the edge of the bed now, looking up at her in a bemused manner. "I, uh, see." He raked a distracted hand through that marvelously thick hair, leaving it in further disarray. "Don't you feel a little...I don't know...unfocused? You seem to try your hand at everything, cooking, carpet-laying, decorating... Wouldn't it be best to master one or two skills instead of trying to do it all?"

One of Catherine's more endearing qualities was that she never bothered reading insults or put-downs into questions directed at her, even on the odd occasion when they were there. It was better to accept things at face value. She smiled genuinely while responding, "Different strokes for different folks. Your area of competence is highly concentrated while mine is spread out. I'm mildly good at all kinds of things, but expert in none. Most of us regular types are. Self-preservation, you know. Nobody's impressed enough by any one of our feats to be willing to wait on us."

She paused in the doorway, the roll of brown paper clamped under an arm and a pencil tucked haphazardly behind an ear. From her vantage point, she looked intently at the network of thought lines permanently pressed into his brow and the smaller little creases radiating from the corners of his intelligent, sherry-warm eyes. "I'll bet you're listed in the *Who's Who of American Scientists*, aren't you?" At his surprised nod, she continued, propping a foot on the doorframe behind her as she spoke. "I thought so. A real Dr. J... So am I," she noted, "—in *Who's Who*, that is—but it's as daughter of Escabito, Martha T." She shrugged. "*She* can't cook an egg, but me—" a hand went to her breast "—maybe I'm no four-star chef, but I'm not bad. Nobody'll ever get ptomaine. Same thing with the rug.

It'll be a decent job, but not spectacular. A professional would be able to pick it out in a minute. Fortunately,'' she grinned impishly, ''I don't number many professional rug-layers among my acquaintances, so I'm all right.''

Jay had yet to break into her monologue, fascinated with just listening and hearing the way her thoughts ran. And Catherine was no longer looking directly at him, but rather at some indeterminate point in space somewhere past his head while she finished. ''The funny thing is, it never oc-curred to me, not for the longest time, that us jack-of-all-trades are just as important as you high-powered, high-IQ types. After all, where would you be without a support group of us more mundane mortals to check and bag your groceries, clean, and cook for you? You'd never get any of your high-faluting figuring done at all.''

Suddenly she snapped to, straightened from her position in the doorway and waved a negligent hand at him. ''So go home and give your cleaning lady a raise. Without her and the garbage man to take the product of her efforts away, the whole system would collapse. Lecture over. Rest well.'' She closed the door gently behind her and was gone. He could hear her humming her way to the john.

Jay lay back on the bed, his large hands clasped behind his head, the ruffled pillow sham carefully set out of his way. The white sand-textured ceiling caught and held his atten-tion as he thought over her offered insights. How much of a Christmas tip had he told his housekeeper to put in the trashman's envelope? He couldn't remember. It hadn't seemed important. His head came up off the bed as he con-templated the south end of her dresser. *Would* a silk flower arrangement finish off the room?

God, he was going crazy.

Chapter Two

Guess who just called?" Iris began talking without even so much as a hello and didn't bother waiting for Catherine to finish unclipping the back screen door before continuing. "My mother-in-law. Can you believe it? She can't stand me and never calls. Absolutely never." The medium-height blonde with the snapping brown eyes popped through the back door as soon as Catherine had it unlatched. With a great deal of dramatic hand and body language enhancing her words, she said, "To be truthful, she didn't actually call to talk to me—she wouldn't spit on me if I was on fire—but Hollis's brother, Juli. It seems my sainted brother-in-law, the Ph.D., is coming for a visit. She seemed to think he was already here. I told her she must be mistaken. I mean, not even a Ph.D. would be dumb enough to drop in unannounced on a woman with three kids, would they? Juli always did have his head in the clouds, but surely he would have called or something—although I have been out at the park all morning—"

"I've got news for you, too, kid." Catherine dropped her own bombshell from her position over the warming tea kettle on the stove. "He's already here."

"You're kidding." Iris blanched and looked comically around the room as though expecting him to pop out from under the kitchen table or out of a cabinet. "Good God, my apartment is a mess. He obviously stopped here if you saw him. Where'd he go? Did he say when he'd be back? How much time do I have to clean the place up?" The vivacious blonde knotted her hand in the ends of her wind-blown mane and looked more closely at Catherine. "He must have rung your buzzer when he couldn't find me. How upset is he?"

"Not to worry. He stopped in here to see if I knew where you were. Poor guy was so tired from driving most of the night, I put him to bed. He's sleeping. Say, you want to be the first to see my bathroom rug? The whole room's really pulling together now. Tea's too hot to drink yet anyhow. Come on."

"Oh, Lord, what am I going to do?" Iris moaned. "I was going to devote the kids' nap time to cleaning. Damn! What'd you do to your bathroom?" She left her tea on the kitchen table and trailed Catherine down the hall, remembering to whisper as she went. "I can't believe Juli let a perfect stranger put him to bed. That doesn't sound like him at all."

"Can't say I gave the poor man much of a choice. I have a tendency to bulldoze when I feel the need, and that guy's eye was giving him hell. He said it was from fatigue, so... What's a seismologist doing in southern Illinois anyway?"

"Now that I do know. Hollis calls him every now and then, so we did know he was down there. I just never expected him to drop in. It's not exactly on his way home. He's very reserved, not comfortable with most people because of his eye, you know. Oh, my, look at this. It really does look nice in here! This just may give me the courage to fix up my own. What a shame the landlord won't replace the medicine cabinet for you.''

Catherine shrugged philosophically and cocked her head to the side while critically eyeing the tub. ''What do you think of the shower curtain?'' she asked.

''I love it. I really do. I never would have thought of this particular color combination, but it's great.'' Iris stepped completely into the tiny room for a closer inspection, but her attention was caught by the mirrored medicine cabinet above the sink instead. '''Mulct'? Oh, my God, you have to be kidding. Maybe you can get your money back. That's worse than the last one I saw. What was it? Oh, yeah, 'pusillanimous.' Now I ask you . . .''

''I liked 'pusillanimous.''' Catherine defended her vocabulary package protectively, forgetting that she had been on the verge of throwing it out only hours earlier. ''What a way to put down a small-minded bigot. 'Sir, your *pusillanimous* tendencies are appalling.''' She glared at Iris, daring her to disagree. ''That was a good word.''

Iris threw up her hands in surrender and started back down the hall. ''All right, I give up. You're nuts, but I am not exactly in a position to cast the first stone. Let me know when Juli wakes up and I'll come fetch him. I need to at least shovel a path through the apartment. A doted-upon bachelor will never understand having to crawl through a jungle of Tinkertoys while inhaling eau de diaper pail. Say, how come you're not at work? I thought you were sick or something when I saw your back door open.''

''I took the late shift for a change. I'm leaving in an hour. How would you like a lacy bare branch with just a bird's nest and a pretty little apricot and brown bird on the wall in

there? And you can't leave until you tell me what a seismologist was doing in southern Illinois."

"I hate fake birds."

"Mmm, I don't know. I saw some pretty nice ones in that
silk flower shop uptown the other day."

"I'd have to see them, I guess. I have to check on the kids.
Tod and John were sleeping, but Emi was up watching Se-
same."

"Then I'm coming with you. I want to hear about Jay."
Catherine followed Iris determinedly out the back door,
crossing over into Iris's kitchen with her steaming tea mug
in hand.

Iris cleaned while she talked, the kid's uneaten sandwich
crusts from lunch were the first to feel the pinch. "Okay, sit
down." She indicated a yellow plastic-cushioned kitchen
chair with a wave of her hand. "I'll get this stack of dishes
started." She squirted a healthy stream of liquid detergent
into a dishpan and flipped on the hot water tap. "Juli explained it on the phone, but he doesn't know any words under four syllables, so I had Hollis translate the basics for me.
There are several small towns downstate that want to go together and put up a dam on one of the tributaries of the
Illinois River and make a reservoir."

Catherine looked up from her cup of tea and frowned.
"They need a civil engineer, then, not an earthquake expert. Aren't they just a tad confused?"

"Patience, my dear, patience." Iris had both hands in a
pan of soapy water. Suds sloshed as she talked. "It seems
there is, in fact, a fault line running for about two hundred
miles from Arkansas up through southern Illinois. Only
nobody knew because the Mississippi has deposited so much
sediment that it was covered up. Now, when you build a
dam and hold back water, the ground underneath becomes

saturated, naturally enough. If the water pressure reaches a certain level, all kinds of nasty things can happen."

"Such as?" Catherine queried with a raised eyebrow.

"Such as the water acting as a lubricant to rock deep inside the fault, reactivating it and causing an earthquake in the area. According to Hollis, some have been as high as six and a half on the Richter scale."

"All of this leading to Jay going down there and doing what?"

"Why do you keep calling him Jay?"

"That's what he said his name was."

"Huh. I've never heard the sainted white sheep of the family called anything but Juli. Maybe his colleagues at work call him Jay, I don't know."

"One can hope. Who'd respect the opinion of a six-foot-four hulky scientist, obviously all male, named Juli?"

"All I know is that both Hollis and his mother call him Juli."

"You should tell them to try to be more charitable in the future."

"You think?" Iris shrugged carelessly, drying her hands on a paper towel and tossing it expertly into the garbage. "It could be worse." She touched her abdomen. "You know, this visit is already really getting to me. My stomach hurts."

"Getting back to the point . . ." Catherine prodded.

"Yes, well, *Juli*—" Iris unkindly emphasized the name "—was called in to beam some kind of sonar waves down deep into the earth and get readings back so that he could help the company doing the work calculate the project's risk to the area. If things go wrong, they don't want to be sued."

"How altruistic." Catherine sighed and rose, stretching as she did so. "Well, duty calls. I have to go change for work. If the temblor prince doesn't wake up before I leave, I'll leave a note telling him you're back and to cross over."

She took her mug from the yellow Formica tabletop on her way out. "See you."

Iris looked at her curiously. "Temblor prince?" she questioned, letting her words hang in the air. "That's a new one."

"Temblor is another name for earthquake, my dear, and it wasn't even one of my vocabulary cards. I just knew it."

"Right. See you."

"Later, gator."

"Uh, excuse me, ma'am. Catherine?"

Catherine was busily banding excess cash in preparation for the Armor truck's arrival when the hesitant voice interrupted her, causing her to lose count. She set down the bundle of five dollar bills, knowing who it would be before she turned around. She hadn't had much exposure to that low-timbered voice, but she'd recognize it anywhere. She turned to face that liquid brown gaze, melting a little as she did so.

"Hi, Jay. You're up." Brilliant. Obviously the man was up. He was standing right there in front of her. "Have a good nap?" Not much better. Clearing her throat, she said, "What can I do for you? Did you need to cash a check or something?"

"Uh, no. Nothing like that." Now Jay cleared his throat and looked discomfited. Catherine waited in polite silence, refusing to add to her list of inane remarks.

"Actually, it seems Iris never got my note saying I was coming. To tell the truth, I found it in my briefcase when I was looking for my pocket calculator. I guess I forgot to mail it. I was working at your kitchen table while she finished up a few little things around the apartment. She was sure you wouldn't mind..." He paused, raising his eyebrows in questioning look.

"No, I don't mind, if that's what's worrying you. Any friend of Iris's, et cetera and so forth."

"Thanks, but I felt awkward and couldn't concentrate so I offered to help. She gave me her grocery list and said I should pick up a few things for her. I think she was trying to get me out from under her feet." Again he cleared his throat. "Unfortunately I'm not much good at this kind of thing. For one thing, it appears eggs come in sizes. Do you know which she buys? And why is everybody in that section opening the cartons and staring at the eggs? What are they looking for? Are they in danger of hatching, or what?"

He stopped and turned his head aside as a bag boy approached the service area. "Catherine Rose, Tracy needs dimes."

Catherine frowned at the interruption. She was finding Julius Gand not only intriguing, but endearing, as well. She could also see that the bag boy was empty-handed. "They told me she was all trained when they transferred her here," she muttered under her breath. "Tom, you know the ropes, even if she doesn't. Tell her that she has to send over five dollars, in exchange for which I'll send down a roll of dimes. In order to keep her drawer balanced she has to buy her change from the booth in exchange for paper money. Otherwise nothing would come out even at the end of the day. I'll be five dollars short and she'll be five over. Explain that to her, will you? Thanks."

Tom the bagger left to explain the facts of grocery store life to Tracy of the number four register. Catherine looked expectantly back to Jay.

"Catherine Rose?" he inquired.

"It's my name." She shrugged.

"But so formal. Was your mother expecting a refined Victorian young lady?"

"If she was, she was in for a big disappointment. I think my friends all use it because it's in such contrast to my actual personality. I tend to be a tad informal and let my hair down on occasion."

"Maybe you should grow it so you could really let it down," he offered as he studied her hair. "I bet it would be gorgeous. It has such shiny highlights, it practically shimmers. Think of a mass of it cascading down your back."

She flushed. Then Jay flushed. It had just popped out spontaneously. Tom the bagger flushed as he held the five dollar bill under the glass partition, finally clearing his throat to draw their attention before the conversation went much further. Wordlessly, Catherine lifted the bill out of his fingers and replaced it with a roll of dimes. He nodded his head and left.

"That will be all over the store in five minutes," she promised in resignation. "I will be hearing remarks about my hair from now till doomsday."

"I'm sorry if I embarrassed you, Catherine Rose."

She gave him a look of inquiry.

"I like it. It fits. Anyway, I'm sorry, but the sentiment stands. You have lovely hair. Now, about those eggs..."

"I'm sorry, too, but I really don't know what size egg Iris uses. Just don't get mediums or smalls. My personal prejudice is they're too little to be of much use. The general rule of thumb is if the price difference is a dime or less, go for the larger size. More than a dime and it's not worth the money. Also, eggs are very fragile, so be sure to open the carton and check that none of them are cracked."

"Is *that* what they were doing over there?"

"You got it."

"This isn't so hard. Ten cents is the cutoff, you say?"

"I did say that, yes."

"Well, onward and upward. Thanks." He took his shopping cart and wheeled it forward, feeling sufficiently girded to face the intricacies of supermarket shopping.

It didn't last long, though, and Catherine was beginning to despair of ever getting the excess tens banded and dropped into the secured part of the safe before Armor's arrival. Something about the man made her consistently lose count every time he showed his face at the customer service area.

"Uh, Catherine Rose?"

"Yes, Jay." In patient forbearance Catherine put down the cash she'd again lost count of. She turned to face the apologetic visage just outside the teller's glass. This would make the third time she'd have to start over on that particular bundle. She hadn't had such a trying day since her initiation into the intricacies of the store's office procedures eight years previously.

"Sorry to bother you, but she's got disposable diapers down here and diapers seem to come in as many sizes as eggs. The child's weight seems to be the determining factor. Would you happen to know how much Tod weighs?"

"No, Jay, I don't." One needed to be as nice as possible to men named Julius. They had enough of a cross to bear. "However, I think we can employ the process of elimination on this one. Newborns would be too small. That leaves mediums, large, and toddlers. Of those, I'd go for the large. Toddy barely toddles and mediums are only a step up from newborns. Take the middle road."

"That's really very good, you know that?"

Catherine shrugged. "As I said, I'm fairly competent in all kinds of things. Some day some guy will get a better than average deal when he gets me."

"Yeah?" Then because he believed her, he asked, "How long's the line now?"

"It's nonexistent at this point," she informed him cheerfully. "Men have trouble seeing past the surface glitz until they mature. I figure if I stick around until one or two of them ripen, they'll discover me just behind the latest over-developed bosom they tried out and lost interest in. Until then, they make good friends."

Jay thought of life outside of tsunami and Raleigh waves to the home a vivacious woman like Catherine Rose might make for a man and swallowed hard. "Would you mind bringing home the diapers? I feel stupid."

"Jay, I won't be leaving here until ten o'clock tonight. And you'd be surprised how many men buy diapers. The checkers all assume it's for their children."

"But I don't have any children," Jay protested.

"*They* don't know that, and Iris may need them." Jay still looked far from convinced. "Look at it this way. It will keep your gorgeous body from being mauled. The women will assume you're a fearless father with a baby. Very few will conclude you have a diaper fetish, believe me. You'd be surprised by the number of men who even buy sanitary napkins."

Clearly astonished, Jay's mouth dropped open. "Whatever for?"

"Here again, we assume it's for the women in their lives, but I suppose it's possible they have some strange fetish or another."

Jay surreptitiously checked the contents of a grocery cart being propelled out the front door by a male driver. "Now I've heard everything," he muttered. "All right, I'll get the diapers. Then I'm getting out of here while I still have a few illusions of life's proper order left."

Catherine looked up from her counting to say good-bye and lost her place again. "Darn," she muttered. "Here's Armor, and I'm nowhere near ready. Double darn, triple darn." She reached for the door and flipped the lock, opening it to the uniformed man with the drawn gun. "Fred, I'm so sorry. This won't take more than two minutes, I swear. Here, put our change order down over there. Can you use my key as well as yours and get the dropped money from the secured part of the safe without me? I only have three thousand more to band and add to it. I'm really sorry. I haven't been this discombobulated since Gary had appendicitis several years ago and left me alone in here to sink or swim."

Fred from Armor finally left, leaving Catherine to breathe easier, but it was only a temporary reprieve. Within moments the store manager arrived from somewhere in the rear, leaning an elbow on the shelf where the customers wrote their checks and asking, "Who's the guy, Catherine Rose? I thought you were saving yourself for me."

Smiling fondly at the balding four-times-over grandfather, Catherine inquired innocently, "What are you talking about, Gary? You know you're the only man for me."

Gary snorted. "Women are so fickle. Leave the storefront for five seconds, and all hell breaks loose. What're you thinking of, letting some guy talk to you like that in a public place?"

Now Catherine was puzzled. What was so bad about being told you had nice highlights in your hair? She was jolted when Gary went on.

"Bedroom eyes, indeed. You didn't fall for an old line like that, did you? I suppose he wanted to show you his etchings, as well. I couldn't believe it when Nick in produce told me that one." He frowned his displeasure. "Catherine Rose, you're like a daughter to me." She could practically see the man gearing up for a lecture. "I've watched you grow up, change from the anxious little girl I hired for part-time checking two days after your sixteenth birthday to the woman you are now. You're old enough to know—"

Catherine gathered just enough of her scattered wits to make a stab at halting Gary's tirade. It was wasted on her anyway; she was still stuck on the "bedroom eyes" part. "Gary, he didn't—" Customers' heads were beginning to turn.

"Can't you see through slick lines like that yet? Mark my words, the guy's only got one thing on his mind, and I can guarantee you, it isn't your intellect or sparkling personality. Furthermore, I don't care how good looking he is—and Helen, who was relieving at the express line then, says he was a real dish—"

"Gary, wait. Hold on. Jay never said I had bedroom eyes. All he said was—"

"So you *do* know his name. It wasn't just a customer giving you a hard time. I thought so. Now you listen to me, Catherine Rose. You're like a daughter to me—"

Wasn't this where she had come in? "He said I had nice highlights in my hair. Do you hear me? That's it. Nice highlights. Brother, this is worse than playing the telephone game. By the time the message comes to you, you get a totally different version than what was actually said. Besides, Gary, you're worse than my own father, you know? I'm a little old for this kind of third degree." She had her pencil stuck behind her ear again and was waving the listing of checks she was trying to run through the adding machine at him in an admonishing fashion.

But Gary was not to be put off. Looking as dignified as possible for a rotund little man in a bright red manager's coat with Vincent Better Foods—Quality For Less in heavy yellow thread script on his pocket, he stated in all seriousness, "Catherine Rose, I've known you since you were sixteen and pleading for a job so you could prove something to your parents. People don't change, Catherine. You've acquired a certain amount of veneer as you've grown older, but you were vulnerable then, and underneath it all, you still are. I don't want you getting hurt, that's all."

The adding machine sputtered into silence as Catherine stopped punching in her numbers. It was a foregone conclusion that the check run wouldn't balance. She looked up, eyes bright and moist. "Thanks, Gary. That's really sweet, but I don't think you have anything to worry about. I don't know him that well, but I don't think Jay's likely to hurt me. He's sort of vulnerable himself."

The store manager looked at her suspiciously, "Who, exactly, is this guy?"

The checks she had cashed for customers added up to fifty-four dollars more than her listing of them. Fifty-four. Divisible by nine. She'd inverted some numbers somewhere down the lengthy list of checks when she'd written them down. Damn. "He's a Ph.D. in one of the earth sciences. Geology, I guess. I'm not sure, as I just met him this morning. But he's very smart, very nice, and very good looking. He's also very sensitive about a small facial muscle tick he's got."

"There has to be more," Gary prodded stubbornly. "What else?"

Well, there was more, but it wasn't going to make him happy. "I'm going to marry him, Gary. Wait and see."

"Catherine *Rose*!" Gary was appalled. "You just said you've only just met. Don't let him rush you off your feet! If he wants you that badly, he'll wait. You have to be sure in something this serious. Marriage is for a long, long time. Ask me, I know. Thirty-three years so far and no end in sight. He can't expect you to—"

"He doesn't know yet."

"He doesn't know y—!" Gary threw up his hands in disgust. "I give up. You've gone off the deep end. You've always been so level-headed. I can't even think what to say right now. I'm going back in the stockroom—but I'll be back," he promised darkly. "Just as soon as I can figure out the proper approach to bring you to your senses."

Catherine laughed and let him go.

She wasn't laughing later, though, when she let herself into her apartment late that evening. She was dead tired and angry with herself for letting the day's events affect her work. It wasn't as though she were in some highly technical field like the rest of her family, she castigated herself. She wasn't called upon for original thinking or precision down to the nth millimeter. All she had to do was minimally keep her mind on what she was doing. It was mostly rote work, which was why she had taken the job in the first place, and today she'd even blown that. Where the hell could she have lost twenty dollars?

Viciously she kicked the door shut. Gratified by the satisfactory echoing protest the rebounding door responded with, she didn't give a thought to her laborious paint job or the black heel mark her rubber-soled shoe had imprinted on the freshly decorated surface. She flung her purse at the nearest chair and watched in moribund fascination as the purse fought for balance on the antimacassared arm, finally giving in to the inevitable and sliding to the floor, dumping its contents as it went.

"Of course," she muttered. "Of *course* it would end up on the floor and not in the chair seat. What else?" There was no satisfaction in stomping in rubber-heeled shoes, so she took them off and flung them against the wall, pleased to find she had aimed at one unpainted as yet.

Hot showers were supposed to relax, but she doubted one would touch tonight's tension. However, due to her limited options, she turned to go down the hall in that direction. She put her hand to her mouth, muffling an involuntary scream as she heard the kitchen door open and saw the lights flicker on almost simultaneously.

A resonant bass anxiously called through the small apartment. "Catherine? What's all the banging? Are you all right? Catherine Rose, where are you?"

Darn, she'd probably woken Iris's sleeping children. What was wrong with her tonight? "I'm right here, Jay. Nothing's wrong, go on back. I'm merely throwing a twenty-four-year-old's version of a temper tantrum."

Then he was filling the kitchen doorway, his body a bewildering contradiction of bulk and grace. "What's wrong? Iris thought you were fighting off a platoon of burglars and gave me your key to come check on you."

Iris knew darn well there were no burglars and that Catherine threw things when she was angry. Burglars were quiet, hence the cat, as in *cat* burglar. They were not boisterous door slammers. The fitting end to a rotten day. She'd never get anywhere if Iris started throwing him at her. Her plan called for tact, diplomacy even. And she didn't have any left at the moment.

"My drawer at work was twenty dollars short, and it's all your fault," she accused abruptly, too upset to notice his startled step backward at her uncalled-for attack. "You'd think I'd never seen a man before, you get me so discombobulated, and I can't find the money anywhere. I've gone over everything with a fine-tooth comb. Even if the Armor driver has time to let me recount the excess cash when he unlocks the secured part of the safe tomorrow, I already know it's not there." She sank disconsolately into the chair and let a propped elbow and hand buttress her sagging head. "I probably gave it away while you were there wreaking havoc on the blood pressure of every woman in the place."

Jay was clearly unused to women speaking their mind quite so directly. He blinked owlishly and stuttered in his amazement. "Me? You're blaming this on me?"

Catherine frowned severely in his direction. "Yes, you. You with the six-foot-four, one hundred ninety-five pound, thirty-four-year-old body. See? I've memorized your stinking driver's license. Men like you ought to be outlawed. You probably leave a trail of destruction wherever you go, and you're so damn blind you don't even realize it."

Jay's work for the Caltech Seismological Lab hadn't prepared him for temblors of this type. He was on shaky ground, and not doing a good job of keeping his balance while he searched for some logical response to a basically illogical argument.

Catherine shot him a disgusted look from eyes crackling with the heat of blue fire. "And don't give me that little-boy-lost look. It's amazing in a man your size, but I bet you could bring out the mothering instincts of a female jackal. And your license is wrong about your eyes. They're not brown. Eyes that liquidy warm shade can't possibly hide under such a bland, generic label. They're more the color of a heated sip of brandy."

"Okay, okay," he soothed, not knowing what else to do with an obviously hysterical female. "I'll request a license correction. Now tell me why you're so upset. Twenty dollars isn't the end of the world. It's not like you're a couple of hundred or a thousand or two off."

"That shows how much you know. Twenty is worse," Catherine sniffed from her chair.

"So tell me, what don't I know?" Jay sat cautiously on the sofa in the far corner of the living room, as far from her as possible. He was a little wary at this point.

Catherine took in his seating choice and closed her eyes. God, she'd blown it. She'd come on much too strong and he'd be retreating from now until the time he left. In despair, she explained the life of head clerk in a grocery store. "I wish it were a couple of thousand instead of twenty." At the surprised way he raised his head to look at her, she hastened to explain. "Don't you see? Nobody would make a mistake giving away something of that magnitude. It has to be a paper error. A deposit you made and forgot to list on your beginning cash tape. A check-run you neglected to write down. Even a register drawer left off the beginning cash tape after you took it in for the evening. The money's there. The problem's in the paperwork, that's all."

She rubbed her eyes tiredly as the adrenaline shot she had been working under eased, leaving her flat, depressed, and more tired than ever. "But an even ten or twenty dollars, that's something else. Two bills sticking together when you cashed a check, a shortchange artist. It could be anything if you didn't have your mind on what you were doing. And I didn't," she stated flatly.

"For which I am somehow to blame."

Catherine looked at him tiredly and sank further into the depths of the chair. "I even checked the safe inventory. There are exactly the number of trays of nickels there should be."

"Nickles being twenty dollars a tray?"

Her hands dangled over the sides of the chair as she responded, "Ten rolls per tray at two dollars a roll."

"Can we go back to the part where this is all my fault? Look at me. Look at my face. I'm the same guy you wouldn't let in this morning because I frightened you." He had leaned forward from his position on the sofa and she could see that his eye was giving him trouble again.

"Oh, Jay." She sighed deeply. "Can't you see that any woman alone in an apartment would have been wary? If I hadn't been so alarmed by the appearance of an unknown male on my three-story-high back porch, I'm sure I would have realized you weren't winking at me purposely. Believe me, it wasn't your eye."

Catherine studied him carefully, cautiously encouraged by the almost imperceptible slowing of the muscle tick. "To tell the truth, I rather like it."

"Oh, come on..." Jay sat back in disbelief.

"No, really. Let me finish. Men—" She searched momentarily for the right word and then plunged in without it. "Men, they *hide* behind these poker faces, you know? Mr. Macho—can't let their feelings show. My dad is one in a million, he lets it all come out in his music. I know what he's feeling by the type of music he plays during his practice sessions. Hours of scales, he's upset; Bach, he's content—and on it goes. It's an unspoken communication. And now you..." She indicated his eye with an eloquent hand gesture. "That eye is an indicator of how you feel, too. Sort of the proverbial window to your soul. It gives me clues to your feelings. You were upset when you came in, now I can see you've calmed down considerably. I like to know where I stand. And I think I'd like to know you," she finally whispered into the room's dim quiet.

Jay sat in his corner of the sofa looking at her for almost a full minute. Then he rose to full height before silently traversing the room to stand towering over her. His eyes never leaving hers, he offered her both his hands, and she took them unhesitatingly. Gently he pulled her to her feet, his probing eyes glued to hers, the silence in the room seemingly unbreakable. Finally he pressed her shining, brown-crowned head into his shirtfront and simply held her close.

Chapter Three

She had been through *magniloquent* and *superciliousness*, and had even managed to work *miscegenation* into a conversation, which hadn't been easy. And, after stalling the Armor man for fifteen minutes while recounting all the excess cash, she had resigned herself to having lost the twenty dollars. Every drawer she'd made up for the next morning's opening had been rechecked to be sure there was the exact prescribed amount in rolled change, singles and fives. She had even triple-checked the pop bottle return slips for the day. The money was decidedly gone, probably given away in a flustered moment dealing with Jay. But it wouldn't happen again, Catherine promised herself. This job was important to her. It was her pink security blanket with satin binding. Here was something she could do easily and well— her home away from a home where she'd lived a frustrated existence in others' shadows. She wasn't going to allow anyone to take those good feelings away from her.

However, the pledge became moot as time rolled on and she didn't see Jay. On the third day S.J.—that was time counted Since meeting Jay, and was roughly similar to B.C. or A.D.—Catherine knew for sure she'd come on too strongly that night in her apartment, parting hug notwithstanding, and had scared him away. Ordinarily she was quite philosophical when a man didn't follow through on calling her and she was surprised by the amount of pain Jay's absence caused. Silly, really. After all, she wasn't without friends. Friends she'd neglected the past few days. She'd call one. If Jay wasn't interested, it was his loss, she told herself roundly. Plenty of other people would be happy to hear from her.

Jay. What did she really know about him anyway? She'd only been with him a small portion of one day. Probably she'd had on her rose-colored glasses. She'd undoubtedly be disappointed if she saw him again. No one's heart had stopped when he had come into the store that she'd noticed. There'd been no bodies piling up in his wake, at any rate. Well, Tracy had drooled a bit, but she was more an object of pity than any real barometer of Jay's appeal.

Catherine thought of how his brawny bigness combined with his slight awkwardness in a most endearing way. She smiled as she realized how ridiculous it was for her to feel protective toward Jay. He outweighed her by a considerable amount and was almost a foot taller. The whole thing was absurd. Yet every instinct in her body told her this was the man she wanted to create a home for. The apricot bedroom flounces could always be changed for something more tailored, even if they were brand new. Ruffles should not be allowed to stand in the way of true love.

Catherine leaned forward and propped her chin on her hand as she surveyed the store's Sunday crowd. It was a good day. There were lines two and three carts deep at every register. Gary would be pleased.

Then there was that brief kiss they had shared. Lordy.

Catherine picked up the mike and ordered three stock boys up front to help bag and move the lines through more quickly. A quick glance at the store's large wall clock told her she was late starting the checker's breaks, as well. She needed to get out on the floor and float from register to register. They couldn't close any down with today's crowd. She took a drawer from the safe and called Gary up to watch the office while she went out and one by one relieved the checkers.

An hour later found only two girls left. That wasn't so bad. So far everyone had cooperated by getting back more or less on time so that the next girl could grab a snack and put her feet up for a few minutes. Catherine approached the express register, prepared to relieve dingy Tracy. Nice enough person. Too bad she was a little dusty up in the attic. Slow was being polite.

She set her drawer on the end of the counter and tried to create order in the jumbled register reading tapes she had collected. Without looking up, she told Tracy, "Take the next order, Tracy, then go on your break. I'll take over while you're gone."

The poor neophyte was clearly puzzled. "But, Catherine, they told me never to allow anybody to touch my drawer."

"That's right," Catherine mumbled over her readings, trying to pair off the beginning and ending for each of the registers she'd been on. "But there are two slots in each register. You're checking on the A drawer. Lock it up and take the key with you. I'll be checking in the B position."

"Uh, okay—if you say so..." Tracy's voice trailed off uncertainly.

There was a certain amount of impatience in the next customer's voice as he broke in requesting, "Pack of Winston regulars—some time today, okay?"

Catherine plumbed the depths of her black smock's pockets, digging for the paper clip she knew she had in there somewhere while Tracy's unsure little-girl voice answered, "Uh, sure—sorry."

She heard the hum of the register in action and the soft whir of the drawer sliding out at the end of the transaction. There was the quiet rustle of paper money being passed back and forth. All of that she ignored. But her head snapped up from her paper-clipping activities and her eyes narrowed suspiciously when she heard the man interpolate, "Oh, wait. Give me back that twenty. I forgot, I'm going to need it. Here, I'll give you this ten and—"

Catherine went into action as money began changing hands in a bewildering fashion. Reaching over the counter, she plucked the twenty dollar bill back out of the man's fingers, silently placed it in the confused girl's drawer and shut the drawer with deadly finality. She looked the man fully in the face and said in a cold voice dripping with Freon, "You need change? Go to the bank. And from now on, we're out of your brand of cigarettes, got it? Permanently out."

Her icy stare never left the weasely looking man who flushed a dull shade but argued anyway, insisting he hadn't gotten the proper change before finally snapping up the pack of cigarettes and leaving. Trying to get her anger under control, Catherine turned back to Tracy and the machine, flipped up the button for the A drawer, locked it, and handed Tracy her key, saying only, "Be back in twenty minutes. I'm running a little behind now."

Tracy was slack-jawed. "But—"

"Not now, Tracy. We'll talk about it later. You know the rules. You don't make change after the transaction has been completed. Now, go."

Mumbling derogatory comments under her breath, Catherine slammed her drawer into the empty drawer of the register. "Lousy, unprincipled scum, think they can—"

"Catherine Rose?"

Catherine's magnificently expressive blue eyes shot up a foot and a half to meet Jay's cautious gaze in return. "Jay!"

His feet shifted as he confessed, "Um, look, I only have a twenty dollar bill, but Iris really needs some milk. I've never heard of a store that wouldn't make change before. Is this common practice in the Midwest?"

Her face took on the warmth and hue of a ripe cherry tomato. "Oh, Jay," she said reproachfully, closing her eyes in momentary disbelief. "You do manage to see me at my aggressive worst. Of course you can buy the milk. Give me the twenty. I'll change it."

"After that last man, I wasn't sure. Do you get much repeat business treating the customers like that? What was that, service without a smile?"

"Jay," she rebuked. "The man was a shortchange artist. A con man. Naturally I was less than civil."

"He was? How could you tell?"

"The line of patter he used isn't exactly new. They prey on young-looking checkers, talking very fast and all the while their hands are moving even faster than their tongue, playing now you see it, now you don't with the money. She's just lucky I was standing here, otherwise her drawer would have been short tonight. By a lot. Ten or twenty dollars." Catherine finished by informing him of how much he owed her for the milk.

He looked doubtfully down at the twenty dollar bill in his hand. "I wouldn't want you to think I'm—"

"Jay, just give me the money. I'll change it for you. I know you're not trying to pull anything," she cajoled, watching the line grow longer behind him.

He looked relieved as he handed it over. "I really don't have anything smaller and I could use some singles."

She was beginning to see that life with a genius would not be without its moments of exasperation. Extending her lower lip, she exhaled a puff of air, blowing her bangs out of her eyes. "I don't suspect everyone of ulterior motives, Jay. Really I don't." She handed him his change. "Here's your receipt. Have a nice day, okay?" She handed him his gallon of milk and waved him on his way, turning to the next customer in line. She wasn't going to make the mistake of falling all over him a second time. She was going to keep her mind on what she was doing. It would be too embarrassing if hers was the drawer to come up short again.

But he was not to be so easily dismissed. "Catherine?"

"Yes, Jay," she sighed. The remainder of the checkout line was getting decidedly restless and she smiled at the unhappy matron waiting next in line. "Be right with you, ma'am." The woman harrumphed her displeasure, obviously doubting the reassurance.

"I was wondering—"

Hurriedly, Catherine interrupted. "We can't talk right now. I've got a lot of people in line and it's getting worse by the second. My break is next. Why don't you wait over by the office? Tracy's due back in just a few minutes."

"Oh, but I don't want to use up your break time—"

"Not to worry." She cut him off and turned her attention to placating the middle-aged lady. She probably shouldn't have bothered. The old bat had twelve items, anyway. Two over the express lane's clearly stated limited.

Tracy was ten minutes late, a record, even for her. Jay had plenty of time to watch Catherine in action. She was impressive. Everyone seemed to have time for a few words with her, yet the line moved quickly and efficiently. The register saw a steady flow of customers who all left with a smile on their face. Catherine was a visual presentation in understated competence, her hands flying from cash register buttons and cash drawer to flipping open brown paper sacks with a single flick of her wrist. Her black nylon office smock wasn't buttoned, and watching her reach for the stack of bags was to watch her cotton T-shirt pull snugly across her breasts, outlining them in intimate detail. When she'd lean for a can, the shirt would gap away. Just enough to present a tantalizingly provocative view of the top creamy-white rise of her high breasts. But the pièce de résistance had to be when both arms were pulled closely together in front of her, one buried in a brown bag while the other flipped cans into the sack for the first to settle properly in place. Now that action pushed her breasts together and gave her a remarkable amount of cleavage.

The time flew by for Jay. He was surprised when Tracy reappeared and Catherine withdrew her drawer from the register and walked toward him. Balancing it against her hip with one hand, she arched an eyebrow and said, "Okay, I'm all yours for the next fifteen minutes. What was it you wanted to know?" She refused to get her hopes up. It wouldn't be a date. He probably wanted to know the difference between orange juice and orange drink, or soy-beef protein mix and seventy percent lean ground beef. Something real romantic like that. So she waited.

Jay didn't disappoint her. "I was wondering . . ." he hesitated, not quite looking her in the eye. "That is, can I do some more work at your kitcen table? It would only be while you're at work. I don't want to disturb you, but I could really use some place quiet to do a few calculations." He blinked at her and seemed exasperated with himself.

Somehow Catherine didn't think it was what he'd intended to say at all. Had he wanted to ask her out and lost his courage? And she realized that despite her good intentions, she'd been holding her breath, hoping that he was going to ask for a date. She felt like flinging her cash drawer against the office wall and listening to the crash echo throughout the store. Neatly categorized pennies, nickles, dimes and quarters would roll all over the store in a massive display of confusion. There was even a half-dollar piece she had taken in that would add to the mess. She saw herself stepping over the whole thing and walking out the double pneumatic doors and never coming back. Why couldn't he want her the way she had instantly wanted him?

She struggled to match his carefully noncommittal tones, responding with a prim smile. "Sure. That would be fine. Get the key from Hollis and Iris. It must be difficult for you to concentrate with the kids around." She could always go home and sit in the chair where he had sat, breathe in the air he had breathed. Maybe there'd be a touch of his masculine scent still hanging in the air—Lord, now she was getting maudlin. What she needed was a package of Twinkies. The narrow little sponge cakes with their sweet filling helped her cope. There was enough sugar in a package of those to give her a high that would last for the rest of the day, at the least.

"Thanks, that's really kind of you." He blinked and smiled a truly devastating kind of smile. One that showed his slightly overlapping, highly polished white teeth to perfection.

Her heart dropped to her feet as she bathed in that smile, and she decided to buy *two* packages of Twinkies. Surely that amount of sugar would see her through. She tuned back into the conversation.

"—are great. I should have come in for a visit a long time ago. Kids accept a person as they are and love them anyway, you know what I mean? It's just that we've got some equipment on a fault line down in Mexico that's starting to put out some interesting data and I'd like to spend some time studying it, as well as finish up the southern Illinois thing. I'm supposed to be on vacation, but you know how that goes." He spread his hands expressively. "There's just no time. I'm going early next week to help another fellow who's working just outside San Francisco. Now that's a fascinating project," he rambled on, not even noticing Catherine's normally perfect posture droop as he discussed leaving. "—of course, he's worked on a few more digs than I have. I was never too interested in that end of the sciences before, you know."

"No. No, I didn't know," she responded, perfunctorily polite.

Jay looked surprised. "Sometimes I forget that we don't know each other all that well. Anyway," he explained, "we'll be digging along the fault line there and trying to read from the juxtaposition of the various earth layers what kind of seismic activity the area has experienced in the periods before we have recorded observations. There may be some kind of pattern there that would help us predict what's to come." He rocked on his heels as he looked down from his great height, seemingly very pleased. "Wouldn't that be something?"

"Really something," she responded dully. She'd never eaten three packages of Twinkies in one sitting before in her life. She'd probably be sick for a month. "Well, I've got to run," she lied. "Get my spare key from Hollis or Iris. See you." And she hurried away. Why couldn't his eyes light up like that over thoughts of her? Why did it have to be some crack in the earth's crust that turned him on? He was so tall, so tan, so handsome. How dare he be insecure? How could all his self-assuredness be limited to his work? He absolutely came to life discussing a temblor. Yet there was such a sense of awkwardness with real people. It would be quite endearing if it wasn't so darn frustrating.

She kicked at a forty-eight ounce can of V-8 someone had knocked onto the floor and left, hurting her toes. Four packages of Twinkies would be unthinkable.

Jay must have lost track of the time. It was the only explanation Catherine could think of when she walked into her apartment at five forty-five that evening to find him still there. Her table and countertop were spread with reams of paper in haphazard stacks and one end of the butcher-block kitchen table supported a portable computer. Jay lounged in a Breuer's chair in front of it, tapping the pink erasered end of a pencil that had never seen a pencil sharpener—rather, it had been whittled to a point with a knife. His briefcase lay open on the floor next to the table and he was evidently deep in thought when Catherine walked through the kitchen doorway and stopped in abrupt amazement.

"What're you doing here?" she asked as she searched for a spot to set her bag of dinner supplies. She settled for one of the stove burners.

"You said it was okay. Don't you remember?"

"Well, sure. But it's almost six o'clock and I know Iris has an early Sunday dinner."

"I wasn't hungry." Jay frowned disgustedly at the computer in front of him and impatiently flicked it off. "I wanted to get this done, but I can't seem to concentrate."

She knew the feeling. "Oh, yeah?" Catherine inquired as she gingerly set eggs into the grooves of her refrigerator door one by one. "What's the problem?"

He was silent so long, she finally glanced over her shoulder and his eyes told her. She held her breath and didn't move, shocked at the gaze of pure hunger that washed over her as his warm brown eyes ate her alive. He did want her. He did. But she was allowed little pleasure in the knowledge as he refused to admit it. "I don't know. I've never had problems like this before."

Catherine turned noncommittally back to her chore at the refrigerator. Now was not the time to rush him. But she only had a week left and she felt panicky. She must make him forget their damaging start. "It'll come, don't push it," she advised herself and looked up, startled to find she had spoken her thoughts out loud.

But Jay took it as being directed to him and agreed with her analysis. "You're right about that. The question is, when? How strong will it be? We have to develop a system that can be used to warn people about these things." She doubted they were talking about the same thing and wasn't about to pursue a clarification.

Trying to decide on the correct course to take with the enigmatic man she wanted so much kept her quiet as she finished putting the groceries away. Finally she folded the bag itself and tucked it under the sink to use for garbage later on. Turning, she found his gaze still on her. Now it was puzzled, as if trying to figure out the fascination she held for him.

Her soft voice seemed to snap him from his reverie. "I'm going to change and wash up. I'll be right back."

"Sure. Don't worry about me." He smiled at her and her heart threw in an extra beat. "You don't have to entertain me."

"That's right. You came over for peace and quiet, didn't you?"

He looked ready to issue a denial and her frustration increased when he shrugged instead. Her lips were tightly compressed as she left the room and headed for the bedroom. Somehow she had to get him to open up, and there was so little time. And she doubted he would respond to another direct confrontation. That first one had not exactly been an unqualified success.

Her hands were jammed into her jean's pockets, her head lowered, and she chewed her lip in indecision as she made her way back down the hall. How would he react to an invitation to stay and eat with her? Maybe he'd bring it up himself.

Somehow she doubted that.

She actually bit her lip when the buzzer high on the wall beside her went off in a discordant squeal. There was little point in using the intercom to check her visitor's identity. Nothing more decipherable than a slight fluctuation in the static level ever came through. So she pressed the security door release button and stepped out her front door to stand on the landing. That way she could see who it was long before they reached her third-floor apartment.

"Bill, what are you doing here?" she questioned in dismay as the handsome medical student bounded up the last flight of stairs.

"I came to see my favorite checker," he responded without the slightest sound of breathlessness in his voice. The man had inexhaustible energy reserves. She was always huffing and puffing by the time she reached the last flight. "I see my timing was impeccable, as usual. I figured I'd given you just enough time to catch your breath after work." He eyed her with obvious satisfaction and nodded to himself. "So grab your purse and let's go."

Bill reminded her of a whirlwind. She loved him dearly as a friend, but there was no peace in his company. "And just where is it that you're off to?" she asked in mild asperity with his good-natured but presumptuous behavior. Her hands rested on her hips, her toe tapped gently against the carpeted top step, and she frowned down on his position four steps beneath her.

He ignored her displeasure and finished the last few steps two at a time to tackle her and carry her back into the apartment over his shoulder, slapping the door shut with the sole of his shoe. "I've got the whole evening free, m'dear. And you and I," he stressed the you, "are going bird-watching. So be a good little girl, Catherine Rose, and cooperate for a change."

She tried to be logical with him as she pointed out, "It's six o'clock. All the little birdies have gone to bed. Now put me down. The blood's all rushing to my head."

"There's where you're wrong."

"It is, too. I can feel it."

"Think of all that extra oxygen being delivered to your brain cells. And I wasn't talking about you. I was referring to the birds. They're out in the early evening feeding just like they are in the early morning. So come on, I've got binoculars and pizza waiting in the car."

"Put me down. I can feel my face turning purple."

"Not until you say yes." Then he wheedled, "If you don't come with me, I'll tell your manager how we met." He'd made the threat before. She had been in a rival chain store and had asked the man next to her to please reach a box of cereal she couldn't quite manage, even on tiptoe. That man had been Bill, and his knee had dislodged four of the large-sized cans of cling peaches from the shelf below as he stretched for her. He had limped for a week and a half and blackmailed her regularly with threats of disclosure. It had been a year ago, and it had been twelve months of never knowing where his antics would lead next.

"Bill, I can't go. I have company." Catherine tried to keep the hair out of her face as he twirled her around. He stopped whirling suddenly.

"Who is it?" he inquired suspiciously. "I *told* Jack it was my turn to work on your virtue this month. Doesn't that man know when to give up?"

Catherine giggled. "It's not Jack. And speaking of not knowing when to give up..."

Bill dumped her unceremoniously on the navy waleless corduroy sofa and caged her there with his arms. "It's Janie. You knew I was coming, didn't you? You're planning on throwing Janie at me again. I keep telling you you're the only woman who can make my temperature—and a few other portions of my anatomy—rise."

Catherine laughed. She had introduced the two and all indications were that things were getting serious. Janie must be busy tonight, leaving Bill at loose ends. She was still laughing when she glanced past his menacing expression to see Jay standing stiffly in the doorway, taking in the scene, his eye blinking wildly and obviously drawing all kinds of patently false conclusions.

"Move out of the way, Bill," she gave a little shove and called, "Jay, come back."

But he was gone, and she heard the back door click shut moments later. With a burst of adrenaline, she pushed the healthy-sized male away and raced to the kitchen. "Oh, darn!" she muttered vehemently. "He's gone. Double darn, triple darn, damn."

His papers were neatly stacked by the computer and there was a scent of an undeniably masculine skin bracer in the air. He must have recently shaved. She didn't know many men who did that late in the afternoon unless they had plans for the evening. Plans that might have included her?

It was the closest Catherine ever came to profanity and Bill would have had to have far less intelligence than it took to get into a top medical school to miss the genuine look of anguish and the wistful touch she bestowed upon Jay's portable computer.

"What's going on, love? Who's gone?"

It took a while for the story to achieve any degree of coherency in Bill's mind, but when it did, Catherine was still blubbering. "That's it. The final straw. He'll go off at the end of the week to read his damn geoglyphics without ever giving me a chance to explain . . ."

"Whoa. Just a second. Hold the phone. What does the guy do for a living? He reads geoglyphics?"

Catherine merely nodded and rubbed her eyes furiously. They had progressed from merely pink to definitive red.

"Geoglyphics. I like it. Is that one of your new words? It has a real ring to it. Any kin to hieroglyphics?"

"No, no. It's not one of my words. It refers to marks in rocks that reveal their geological past. Well, actually, I did see it in a vocabulary book when I was out looking, but I didn't buy that one. I got the cards instead. His next project is digging some place along the San Andreas fault to try to read the seismic history of the area by the juxtaposition of the soil layers. Fascinating, huh?"

"Well, actually, no. Not to me. That's why I went into medicine and not geology. Vivisection, now that's fascinating.

Catherine sniffed, "Well, *he* thinks it's fascinating, and *he's* leaving the end of this week to go pursue said fascination."

"Now, Catherine Rose, just slow down," Bill soothed. "It'll all work out, you'll see. I'll go over and explain everything. How would that be?"

"No, don't you dare. There isn't anything between us yet that would merit explanations of boyfriends, don't you see? It's more a feeling on my part that something might have come of the evening. If you go over and start justifying your existence, it will only make me look overly aggressive again."

Bill was having a little trouble following her line of reasoning, but laughed out loud at Catherine's worry. "The role of female barracuda just doesn't suit you, love. I have trouble picturing you in it at all."

"Stick around, kid," Catherine muttered glumly. "Something happens to me around him and I practically throw myself at his feet. I want to wrap my arms around his ankles like leg chains and never let him out of my sight. Can you imagine that?"

"Frankly, no." Bill studied her morose figure, which drooped over a kitchen chair, and the finger that absently rubbed the coarse texture of the computer's plastic sheathing. "However, I happen to know that there's nothing like pizza for unrequited love pains. Come on, ours is waiting in the car. We'll go up to the Botanical Gardens in Glencoe and I'll look for birds while you cry on my shoulder. My only request is that you don't get the pizza wet. I can't stand soggy pizza."

Chapter Four

Her time out with Bill helped Catherine put things into better perspective. This whole thing was silly. What chance was there for a woman to make herself indispensable to a man in a week and a half? Slap-dash, hasty courtships and marriages ended in the divorce courts more often than not, she was sure. There just wasn't enough time, not even if he professed undying love and devotion in the next five minutes or so, to be sure that their attraction was of the enduring kind. And besides, she'd never believed in one Mr. Right per female anyway. The way she saw it, you met somebody—probably by chance—who was at a similar place and time in their life as you and bingo—things clicked. Logically the thing for her to do was wait for a more likely and local candidate.

She told herself all of that while she tried to sleep. She flopped onto her stomach and restlessly punched the pillow underneath her stomach as she told herself the same tale yet again. The phosphorescent arms of her bedside clock gleamed a sickly luminescent green in the dark. One-thirty in the morning, and sleep was certainly being elusive. Where was the Sandman when you needed him?

"Shoot," she muttered under her breath. Off in the distance, a child wailed in the night. Catherine plucked the pillow out from under her stomach and jammed it over her head in an attempt to block the noise.

The pillow was totally ineffective as the wailing intensified. Gradually the child's cry took on a desperate tone and she realized it was quite nearby. Unless she missed her mark, it was right next door. It had to be Tod. Had Iris and Hollis gone deaf? Why didn't one of them go in and placate the child? They had neighbors who were trying to get some rest, for crying out loud.

Catherine squirmed impatiently in bed. Her skin had become hypersensitized since Jay's arrival. She could actually feel the quilting lines in the mattress pad beneath the percale sheet. Talk about the princess and the pea! Now she tingled all over. She'd taken to imagining Jay's hands on her at the oddest, most inopportune times. Scrubbing down in the shower had become an almost erotic experience. Impatiently she checked the clock. Five minutes had gone by and Toddy was still screeching his dear little head off.

After ten minutes Catherine threw her pillow across the room. It knocked some paperbacks off the round table next to the wicker rocker and landed propped mockingly against the far wall. Catherine glared at the mess. Flinging the sheet back, she stalked from the room, intent on waking somebody next door even if she had to shake the door from its hinges.

That wasn't necessary. As she reached the back porch she could see that every light in the place was blazing. Before she could knock, Jay entered the kitchen clasping a livid, squalling child in one arm, his free hand blocking the ear closest to Tod's mouth. He was looking decidedly frazzled. He must have been pacing the floors for some time. His eye was twitching to beat the band.

Jay looked up when she tapped on the door's glass pane and an expression of pure relief broke across his face. Crossing the room, he manipulated the latch one-handed and swung it open, commenting as he did so, "Am I glad to see you. What's wrong with this kid?"

Catherine studied Tod closely. Whatever was wrong wasn't readily apparent. His head was mottled purple but was still hooked onto his shoulders. His arms and legs looked firmly attached, although it was hard to tell with all the flailing. "What do I know about kids? Where are his mother and father? Parents are supposed to know what to do at times like this."

"They're not here," Jay stated more than a little desperately. "They went to the hospital about an hour ago. This little guy woke up twenty minutes ago, and all hell is breaking loose. Don't you have *any* ideas?"

Catherine looked at him, stunned. "The hospital? Jay, what's going on?"

"They think maybe Iris has appendicitis. Hollis took her over to be checked out. In the meantime, I'm going stone deaf. Maybe Toddy caught appendicitis and we should run *him* over to the hospital, too." The suggestion was made almost hopefully.

Catherine looked the child over critically. Appendicitis wasn't catching as far as she knew. And he didn't seem to be in pain, more upset. "Maybe he's wet," she offered dubiously.

Jay grabbed the suggestion eagerly. "I should have thought of that. Do you know how to change a diaper?"

"Well, it can't be all that difficult," Catherine returned pragmatically. "Where does Iris keep the baby powder, diapers, and things like that?"

"Back here." Jay strode purposefully toward a bedroom, delighted at the prospect of deliverance.

"Not much point in worrying about waking Johnny up," he muttered as he flicked up the light switch in the room the two tykes shared. "This kid has been shrieking loud enough and long enough to wake the dead."

Sure enough, Iris's four-year-old middle child was sitting Indian-style in the middle of the bed. As they came in, he calmly reached over to the desk at the end of his racing car-shaped bed and retrieved the smallest pair of wire-rimmed spectacles Catherine had ever seen and propped them on his nose. "Hi, Catherine," he said, blinking owlishly in the bright light.

"Hi, yourself, Tiger. What do you suppose is wrong with your brother?" she asked conversationally, not really expecting a reply. "He sure is mad over something."

Johnny blinked twice before stating matter-of-factly, "Yeah, he gets that way when he can't find his blanket."

"What?" Catherine did a double-take.

"He wants his blanket," Johnny repeated. "He always gets stinkin' mad when he can't find it."

"That's right," Another small voice piped in from the open bedroom door. Little Emily, in her Strawberry Short-cake nightgown, made an appearance. "You should see him when Mom takes it away to wash it."

Jay and Catherine gaped at the two small children. "If you knew what was wrong," Jay inquired disbelievingly, "why didn't you say something before this?"

Emily shrugged and John defended himself self-righteously. "You never asked."

His logic was irrefutable. They hadn't. Jay swallowed before asking in a small voice, "I don't suppose you know where this infamous blanket is?"

Johnny pointed toward the crib in that same deliberate manner. "Probably fell behind his bed. He can't reach it when it does that."

"That's why he's crying?"

John nodded while Catherine pulled the animal-decorated crib away from the wall to retrieve the blanket. The stuffed plastic bird mobile wobbled wildly in the air as she handed the frayed crib blanket to the blubbering baby. Fascinated, she and Jay both watched as his sobs died away and he tried to catch his breath. Finally he hiccuped twice and lay his head against Jay's shoulder while his thumb and forefinger worked the blanket's satin binding back and forth. He popped his other thumb into his mouth in a final gesture of self-pacification.

"I don't believe it," Catherine murmured. Jay sank in relief into the nursery cushioned Boston rocker. Tod was asleep almost immediately, worn out from his frustrating encounter with the dim-witted adults in his world.

They slipped from the room moments later and tucked Emily back in with her stuffed Annie doll and John with his red fire truck before retreating to the kitchen. Catherine flicked on the flame under the tea kettle. "I don't believe it," she repeated, reaching for the two mugs sitting on the sink drainboard. "All we had to do was ask." She laughed and shook her head while routing through the cabinets for some tea. "I suppose he's been told not to interrupt or something, but honestly..." Her voice trailed off on a giggle.

"At least you had the sense to question them. I can't believe I didn't think to do even that much. I'm really useless at stuff like this." Jay shook his head disparagingly. "I probably have permanent hearing loss."

"Don't be so hard on yourself," Catherine encouraged. "You're just not around kids that much, that's all. You'd get the hang of it soon enough if you had one of your own."

He denied it almost mournfully. "I don't think so."

"Well, I think I might," Catherine stated positively as she leaned back against the counter, absently dipping her teabag up and down in the mug of steaming water. Silently she watched Jay blink and shift his feet. She already knew him well enough to know he was working up to something.

"Catherine—" The thought was lost as he was interrupted by the intrusive harsh ring of a telephone jangling on the wall three feet from his shoulder.

"Hello? Oh, good, Hollis, it's you. What's the verdict? No, I wasn't asleep. Yes, I guess it was lucky to have caught it in time.... I don't see how I could stay that long. What about Mother? ...Yes, I guess I can be rather dense at times. I didn't realize there were hard feelings.... Ten days you say? I had planned on leaving Friday. I'll have to see what I can work out.... No, no. Don't worry. I'll work something out. Maybe I can get some paperwork shipped here or something. Not to worry. Give Iris a big hug when you can.... Right. Talk to you."

Jay hung up the phone and turned a very calculating look on Catherine.

"Catherine," he began determinedly, and Catherine knew what was coming. She'd be a fool not to, the way his eyes gleamed and had her pinned to her spot against the countertop like a butterfly to an examining board.

"Jay, these are my only two days off all week, and I don't know anything more about children than you do," she began defensively.

He brightened considerably. "You have today and to-morrow off?"

Uh-oh. That had been a tactical error. She nodded glumly. "Monday and Tuesday are the slowest days of the week in a grocery store. That's why I get them off. But I have plans."

He glowered. "Lover boy Bill coming back to wrestle you around the living room?"

"Jay, he's just a friend. Bill's wildly in love with a girl I fixed him up with a few months ago and she was busy this evening. Horsing around is just his way. Doesn't mean a thing."

His doubtful expression said it all. "That's probably what he wants you to think while he gets a cheap thrill. You should have screamed—"

"I could send a bill," she offered impishly. "Then nobody could say it was a *cheap* thrill."

"Catherine Rose—"

"My, how formal all of a sudden!"

Jay was not going to allow her to sidetrack him. "Catherine, I *need* you," he pleaded.

Wouldn't it have been nice if that *need* was a less conditional *need*? she thought to herself.

"You couldn't be so heartless as to leave me at the mercy of three little kids, could you?" He paused to gauge the effect of his words and was not overly encouraged by the expression on her face. He tried again. "Catherine, I'm a scientist. Look at my eye. You can see what a wreck I am over this, but I can hardly turn down my own brother while his wife is ill. Come on," he wheedled. "Pretty please?"

Catherine crossed her arms defensively over her midriff in a posture her father referred to despairingly as hugging her buggy, and tapped her toe reflectively while she studied the eye in question. Finally she stated, "I think you're doing that on purpose to play on my sympathies and control me. I have to say I don't like being manipulated."

Jay was clearly wounded at the accusation. "If I were going to manipulate a woman, believe me, it would not be with a spastic eye."

She felt bad, not only for the unthinking words, but Iris *was* her friend after all. She *should* help out; it was only neighborly—and also too fortuitous a situation to pass up. "Oh, all right. Give me the morning to get a few things done around the apartment and I'll help you with lunch and the rest of the afternoon."

"Thank you from the bottom of my heart, Catherine Rose." The sentiment was heavily laced with relief.

Gratitude, she guessed, had him bounding out of the chair and toward her. Catherine straightened from her semi-slouch and looked up with startled eyes as he pulled her into his embrace.

"You're sure that character tonight was just a friend?"

She nodded mutely.

"Well, I may not manipulate people with my eye, but I bet I can show gratitude at least as well as that jerk."

Catherine was thrilled by this small sign of jealousy and teased, "You're going to whirl me around the room?"

He shook his head in a negative fashion and rested one hand flat on the small of her back while the other supported the base of her skull. It certainly looked to her as though he had every intention of kissing her.

"I thought you were shy and retiring on account of your eye," she whispered, locking her hands around his neck.

"You've assured me I'm overly sensitive," he murmured back, his mouth only a fraction of an inch over hers, his breath a warm zephyr wreaking havoc on the sensitive skin of her face and neck. "And as long as it doesn't seem to bother you, I thought I might get in a little work on my technique. Wouldn't want to lose what little I had, you understand.''

His lips gently closed on hers and Catherine was lost in a world of their own making. Her fingers twined themselves into his thick hair. She had to stand on her tiptoes to do it. Her neck ached from craning, but she didn't care. The arm around her back gradually tightened, making it hard to breathe. It didn't matter. Nothing mattered. Nothing except the wonder of the deepening kiss. His tongue cajoled its way into her mouth's warm recess, meeting minimal resistance. Her lips opened and his tongue swept in. Catherine curled her toes in heady pleasure.

Jay straightened to his full height, keeping her held against him. ''Catherine,'' he ground out.

She clung to him, loving the intimate knowledge the position gave of her effect on him.

''God, Catherine!'' Her name was more of a plea now.

Catherine responded in kind. *''Jay,''* she whispered. ''From the first moment I opened my back door to you, I thought it could be like this between us. I didn't think you'd give it a chance, though.''

She doubted he heard her low murmurings. He was too engrossed in investigating the pink shell of her ear. Any awkwardness she'd noticed in their earlier dealings was gone. He pulled her further up into his arms and in as blatant a male move as she had ever seen, he literally carried her off, putting her down on the overstuffed gold and yellow Herculon sofa in Iris's front room.

He eased down next to her, facing her, searching the depths of her languid blue eyes one minute, placing his warm lips over hers the next.

Wonder swamped her. His body, clad only in faded cotton pajama bottoms presented few obstacles to her hands with their sudden case of wanderlust. She let them prowl through the luxuriant silky mat of thick hair that prickled her breasts through her own light nylon nightgown and robe. She searched out the flat male nipples, almost hidden in the thicket. His hands tightened momentarily on her shoulders, and she could feel a light shudder course through him.

"You are incredible, woman," he told her on a heavy breath. Her warm acceptance of his initiative had given him confidence. He held her with one arm while the opposing hand closed a little awkwardly over her breast. It was fortunate he'd been unsure of himself and locked in his work these past years. Had he had more experience, she'd have been in serious trouble. As it was, Catherine was still minimally aware of her surroundings. The flopping of the lightweight, too bright floral drapes hanging in the open windows almost, but not quite, masked the sound of a key scratching against the front doorplate as it searched for the keyhole. Hollis was back from the hospital. Quickly Catherine sat up. Her breath was uneven and her hair in disarray. She looked at Jay. His hand was flung over his forehead and his eyes were closed, his disappointment clear.

She raked a hand nervously through her hair. If Hollis saw her like this, it would take him all of two minutes to figure out what he'd interrupted.

"Slip out the back, Catherine Rose," Jay advised quietly. "I'll see you tomorrow."

He kissed her quickly and hiked his pajama pants a little higher on his lean hips before he went to stand by the front door, waiting for her befuddlement to clear and her escape made, before lifting the chain guard Hollis was quietly cussing out and letting his brother in.

Monday morning dawned clear, bright and warm, but Catherine was so tired she missed the sunrise. Shortly after eight o'clock, she stirred. A glance at her bedside clock radio told her it was well past her normal rising time and she swung her legs over the side of the bed to sit up. She felt fuzzy and sluggish. Compared to her normal 6:00 a.m. rising, she'd slept half the morning away. Rumpling her hand sleepily through her shiny shoulder-length brown hair, she gave herself a push off the bed and shuffled her way to the bathroom, where she peered drowsily into the mirror. Unable to face the reflection, she turned away and fumbled in the box inside the medicine cabinet.

Persiflag. Oh, for heaven's sake. A light flippant style of conversation or writing; banter; raillery. She flipped the card directly into the wastebasket, not bothering to tape it to the mirrored glass, and picked up *animadvert*. That one followed the first. She didn't even bother to read the definition. She'd never use a word like that. Instead she flipped on the shower, determined to dispel her system's lethargy somehow.

Lathering herself with soothing yellow soap froth, the spray of the shower masked the sound of the frantic pounding on the back door. She froze under the pelting stream, however, when the banging on the bathroom door began.

Jay's voice called through the wood paneling, "Catherine Rose! Are you in there?"

Wasn't it wonderful what a knowledge of scientific deductive reasoning could do for you?

Catherine turned the shower taps off and cowered behind the shower curtain, as though Jay was blessed with x-ray vision. "Yep, it's me all right. What do you want, Jay?" She reached an arm out from behind the curtain and snared one of her new plush towels, hurriedly rubbing herself dry.

"I need you, Catherine."

Her heart gave a leap.

"I was trying to give them breakfast, but all hell is breaking loose. Can you come and see what's wrong? How bad can my scrambled eggs be, for God's sake?"

Her heart sank in disappointment. He didn't need *her*. He just *needed* her. Darn. "I wouldn't know, Jay. I've never had them," she called back through the paneled door, relieved to at least have her underwear on now as she hadn't locked the door. *Who could walk in on your shower when you lived all by yourself, after all? People you gave keys to in moments of temporary insanity, that's who,* she thought. "Go on back and referee for a minute. I'll be there shortly."

"I need you now." His voice had that same slightly desperate quality she'd first heard the night before.

"You can't have me now. I'm not dressed," she advised as she tried to hop one-legged into a pair of khaki walking shorts. "I'll only be a minute or two, I promise."

"Catherine, I wouldn't notice if you were a nude ringer for Marilyn Monroe at this point. Just come. Tod's face is turning purple and even if it were Lent—which it's not— breathing is not a good thing to give up." She could almost hear the muscle twitch in his eye pick up speed as he talked.

She lost her flamingo-stanced balance and had to steady herself on the toilet tank. Finally she had the shorts on. She pulled up the zipper with a sigh of relief and reached for her cap-sleeve aqua blouse that could be as decent or un as you wanted, depending on how tightly you adjusted the drawstring at the neck opening.

She tugged it on and pulled open the door, stepping into blue flip-flops as she did so. "All right," she gasped. "Now what's the problem?" Her fingers tried to rake the tangles from her wet hair and she patted it with a towel as she spoke. Without the muffling influence of the door and cascading water, the distant cries of real unhappiness were clearly audible.

"Just come," Jay directed impatiently. "I need an interpreter." To ensure her compliance, his fingers girdled her wrist and he pulled her along with him as he started down the hall.

"I have to dry my hair. Surely you can cope for five more minutes."

"Catherine, I'm a desperate man. I will personally pay for a team of beauticians to undo any damage done to your hair if you will just come *now* and decipher the problem."

"Why are you giving them breakfast now anyway?" she questioned grumpily, allowing herself to be tugged down the hall. "You're two hours late. I happen to know those kids rise with the sun."

"So we're running a little behind this morning. *Come on!*"

The sight greeting her in Iris's kitchen was not pretty. The kids had evidently risen with the sun and Jay simply hadn't heard them. Little Emily must have taken it upon herself to try making breakfast and breakfast cereal was sprinkled over ninety-five percent of the room's flat surfaces. Milk had been sloshed onto the countertops. The cereal there had turned to mush. Eggshells from Jay's attempt at scrambled eggs lay in half-hardened pools of egg albumen, and were already sticking to the countertop like glue.

Catherine closed her eyes in momentary disbelief. "Lord save us all," she muttered under her breath.

"Amen," Jay concurred heartfeltedly.

Toddy stopped screaming long enough to study her doubtfully. Catherine knew she didn't have much time before he started in again. She quickly gathered the plates with their cold rubbery contents and dumped them in the garbage. Taking out a fresh pan, she lobbed in a pat of butter and hastily set it on the stove while casting a surreptitious look over her shoulder at Tod. So far, so good, atlhough his lower lip was still jutting out threateningly. She quickly cracked fresh eggs into a bowl, watching as the number of golden yolks grew. Adding a dab of milk, salt, and pepper, she whisked them up with a fork and dumped the mess into the heating frying pan. The mixture sizzled happily as it hit the pan.

"Why'd you throw mine out?" Jay interrogated, watching as she lay a wet cloth over the hardened egg albumen on the countertop. "If you're just going to make the same thing over again, what's the point? I don't think they like scrambled eggs."

Catherine stirred the eggs with a flick of one wrist as she sponged soggy cereal off the counter with the other. "I know Iris feeds them scrambled eggs. I think maybe yours had just been out of the pan too long and were cold," she lied. From what she had seen, his had been lost from the moment he had opened the refrigerator door. "Why don't you try to sweep some of the cereal off the floor? It's getting stepped on and Iris will have ants before she knows it."

Jay looked down and was surprised by the sight. Reaching for the broom, he commented, "I didn't really notice how much had spilled, I guess."

"It's just that it's so sugary—"

"But ants up here on the third floor?"

"Believe it. Worse yet, cockroaches. They're very difficult to keep out of apartment buildings."

Tod's lower lip was assuming threatening proportions and the fork in his little fist banged the tabletop ominously. Catherine grabbed plastic plates from the cabinet and hurriedly spooned the creamy egg mixture, done to perfection, onto them. "It's coming, Toddy. Hang in there. Here...they...are!" She made an airplane noise as she delivered one small plate in front of each small child. Catherine beamed triumphantly at the cherubic-faced one-year-old and leaned to help him with a forkful. "Don't they look good, Tod? Open wide and Catherine will help you," she cheerfully directed. She was more than a tad taken aback when Toddy looked at the eggs, then fixed a baleful eye momentarily on her before again bellowing at the top of his lungs and shoving the plate of eggs as far as possible.

Neither Emily nor John had touched theirs, either. She rescued Toddy's eggs from the brink of the table and her bemused look slid back and forth between the plate and the crimson-faced little boy. She had been so sure...She knew there was nothing wrong with *these* eggs.

"Maybe we ought to try French toast," Jay suggested doubtfully, emptying the dustpanful of cereal into the garbage. "I'm telling you, these kids just don't like scrambled eggs."

But Catherine had *smelled* them cooking many a warm morning, she *knew* they ate them. Her glance fell on little brown-haired Emily. The direct approach. That was the ticket. It had inadvertently worked the night before. "Emily," she said. "What's wrong with the eggs? Why is Toddy screaming like that?"

Innocent blue fixed on anxious blue as Emily calmly informed her, "Toddy's cryin' cuz he doesn't got any ketchup on his eggs." As an afterthought, she added, "Johnny likes ketchup, too," and then further appended, "and so does I."

Jay ground his teeth in frustration, but Catherine was too relieved to be upset. She merely grinned, "Oh, you does, does you?" She laughed at Emily and John's solemn nod and turned to lean into the refrigerator, searching for the familiar red bottle. "Okay, ketchup it is, then." And she poured the thick red sauce in a puddle in the center of their eggs.

Toddy turned the tears off like a spigot and Emily happily picked up her fork. John studied it momentarily over the top of his little bifocals before doing the same.

Jay simply stared in disbelief. "I don't believe it," he muttered under his breath. He raked a hand exasperatedly through his luxuriant sherry-toned hair, leaving it sticking up at odd angles, before turning to Catherine. "You must be the eighth wonder of the world," he declared. "I'm still not sure how you figured it out, but I'm certainly glad that today's your day off." He enveloped her in a crushing bear hug.

The man didn't know his own strength, she thought as she gasped. And in her opinion, spending the day with him would be a mixed blessing at best. True, she'd get to spend time with Jay, but they'd be well chaperoned by the gruesome threesome.

Motherhood was something she had anticipated easing into, one child at a time, with nine month's advance warning. Three small children simultaneously dumped into one's lap might be a little more than even a slightly above average type could cope with. She'd lucked out twice. How often would it be possible for Emi or John to pinpoint the causative agent of little Toddy's tears? And what about Jay himself? Since Toddy's tears could not be charted on a seismograph, she was unlikely to receive any real aid from him. But then, she noted on a sigh, he didn't have to be useful. Just being able to look at him and stay in his company all day would be gratifying enough. She shook her head. Easy does it. God seemed to be on her side and kept throwing them together. She would blow it all if she started ripping off his clothes and jumping his bones the way she felt like doing. She couldn't afford to scare him off again.

Yet this odd aching, this unfamiliar longing so filled her that she would have to do *something* to keep herself occupied. Something active that would keep the kids from whining and prevent her from throwing herself at Jay. She had to program the day, fill it from now until bedtime.

"I know," she stated decisively. "When we're done cleaning the kitchen, we'll pack a picnic lunch and go to Santa's Village. Won't that be fun?" she questioned brightly.

Chapter Five

Catherine pushed Tod in his stroller while Emi demurely held on with one well-behaved hand. John was as on top of the world as he was likely to get at his tender age, riding six feet off the ground straddled across Jay's broad shoulders. *Why, we could pass for a family,* Catherine mused as they strolled past a reflective surface on their way to the petting zoo. She smiled up at Jay. He grinned back and reached for her hand, placing his over hers on the stroller handle.

Familial images deepened over the back of a dusty white-and-brown goat loose in the petting zoo's yard. John handed Tod some of the twenty-five cent a packet feed and Toddy held his hand out bravely. But when the goat decided to take him up on the offering, Toddy screeched and panicked. As one, Catherine and Jay dropped down to Toddy's level to offer comfort. Their eyes met and held over the animal's head. Catherine hugged Tod to her, her eyes never leaving Jay's burning gaze. They rose together, Toddy's sturdy little legs straddling Catherine's waist. Jay used a muscular arm to impulsively squeeze her in a very natural gesture and then left it draped across her shoulders, effectively lashing her to his side.

"You know," he commanded, sounding almost surprised. "What you said this morning...you could be right. I could develop a feel for this kind of thing. This hasn't been the nightmare I anticipated." He looked to her for confirmation.

"This is your basic baptism by fire," she commented with a genial grin that lit up her face in a way that caused Jay to stare. "If you can make it through a day with three active kids, being presented with them one at a time ought to be a piece of cake."

Jay studied her. Wisps of fine brown hair had escaped the general tousled mass, framing her face. Her eyes were lit with the gentle glow of a burning candle, and they heated the space between them with their warm blue flame. Her cheeks were flushed and healthy looking. They were covered with the fine sheen induced by a day's exertion under a strong summer sun. "You're not a Catherine," he stated while tentatively touching a lightly freckled, slightly burnt cheek. "Nor a Catherine Rose. There's too much life and vibrancy in you for such prim and proper names. You're a Rosie," he informed her positively. "With a red rose's vibrant hues and its deceiving surface fragility, but mostly its flair and capacity for transmitting pleasure to its beholder. Just like Mr. Rogers told Toddy this morning, You are special, Miss Rosie." He kissed her nose and clamped her once more to his side.

Jay then took them off to find an Italian ice stand, but Catherine's enjoyment in the day ground to a stop. It had felt so right under his wing, sort of protected and cherished. Twined together as they were, they created a unit, a whole. But his intimate words and gestures had only served to remind her that it was all just an illusion. He was leaving in just a few days. *Leaving.* She'd never feel truly complete again. Not like she had before meeting him.

Jay seemed not to notice how quiet and introspective she had grown. His own volubility increased as he became more secure in his unusual role. They packed the blue denim stroller along with the pitiful remains of the well-received picnic lunch into the small space behind the third seat of his mocha-colored rented Voyager. The children were barely able to stay awake long enough to be buckled into their safety seats. Catherine and Jay could have been alone in the car for any interference the occupants in the rear offered as they swayed and nodded deeper into the padded upholstery.

Thank God for bucket seats, Catherine thought gratefully as she patted the cloth seat. At least his arm could no longer drape her shoulder, making her wish for things that would never be.

Jay glanced over momentarily before returning his attention to the windshield and the blacktopped road ahead. "Did you say something, Rosie?"

She wished he wouldn't call her that. There was an intimacy about a private nickname that would make the loss when he left that much harder. "No. Nothing."

"Oh, I thought you did."

"No."

He glanced over quizzically and she folded her hands into her lap and stared at them. There was a strange phenomenon taking place. Jay was loosening up, becoming almost loquacious, one might say, obviously feeling more and more at home with her and the children. His eye had hardly been noticeable since the ketchup and egg incident at breakfast, whereas Catherine's sense of awkwardness and tongue-tiedness, a new sensation for her to be sure, was growing in inverse proportion to Jay's volubility. She almost jumped when his huge hand covered both of her clenched fists and settled into her lap with them.

"What's wrong, honey?" he questioned softly as he steered one-handed around a construction barricade.

Lord, he'd called her "honey." Heart palpitations came thick and fast with that.

"I thought you enjoyed yourself today. Is there something at home you should have gotten done? I'll give you a hand once Hollis gets back," he offered. When she didn't respond due to her taking deep breaths to control her heart rate, he continued more tenuously, "Or is it me? Did being with me and the kids embarrass you?"

How could he not know why she was upset? Didn't he feel any of the melancholy the illusory quality of the day had left her with? "Being with you does not embarrass me, Jay, believe me," she said with such obvious sincerity that Jay smiled at her in relief. Catherine smiled back before glancing out the windshield. Her foot pressed an imaginary brake on her side of the car. "Jay, look out!"

Quickly Jay's eyes flashed back to the road and he swore and stood on the brakes, missing a car that had shot out from a side street by fractions of inches. The brakes of the car behind them howled in protest, but there was no jolt following the screech. "I thought this was a through street," Jay grumbled as he cautiously set the car once more in motion, both he and Catherine clearly shaken by their near miss.

"It is," Catherine assured him breathily. "That guy must've found his license on the bottom of a box of Cracker Jacks. He came right through that Stop sign."

"It was a woman," Jay assured her chauvinistically. "No man would ever do anything so stupid behind the wheel of a car."

"What a ridiculous thing to say!" Catherine huffed indignantly. "It was a man! I had a clear view. After all, he was only two feet away from me at the time he cleared the front of the car."

"Men think too much of their cars to endanger them like that."

"For a man of science, that's a perfectly preposterous hypothesis," Catherine blustered anew.

"I love it when you get all excited," Jay returned irrelevantly. "Your eyes flash blue fire and your cheeks get all pink and heated."

A little dose of self-assurance certainly went a long way with this man. Talk about disconcerting! "That can be accomplished in other ways besides generalized slams at over fifty percent of the world's population. Honestly, men can be so...so..." Jay laughed and Catherine looked at him suspiciously. "You were trying to get a rise out of me, weren't you?"

"It got your mind off whatever you were brooding about, didn't it?"

"You are an unscrupulous person."

"I'm beginning to suspect that's true," he agreed.

"I'll consider myself warned."

He nodded in satisfaction. "You do that. Now about those other ways you mentioned of getting your cheeks all pink and heated."

"Jay," she asked in irritable exasperation. "Why are you baiting me this way?"

Jay was surprised by the touch of hurt he heard underlying the words. He'd only been teasing.

"This has been going on all afternoon, and it's making me crazy."

"I knew there was something bugging you. Come on, Rosie, fess up."

"Don't call me Rosie!"

"Why not?" he questioned reasonably.

"Look," she began in a bid to explain herself before she twisted her small opal earring right through to the opposite side of her earlobe. "When you do things like that, and tease me about ways to get my cheeks to flush, can't you see it's like an open invitation for me to take you seriously? And the last time I tried to do that, I scared you away for three days!"

"That's not true," he protested self-righteously. "I just wasn't quite sure how to handle it. I've never been openly pursued before. I thought you'd be disappointed with me if I let you get too close, and I didn't feel like being rejected. It happened in graduate school. And again at the institute. Both of them used me to get through a difficult project they were stuck on and then, *goodbye, Charlie*. I figured my brain was all I had to offer a relationship. But we've had a decent time today, don't you think? And I sure can't help you with any knotty grocery store or decorating problems."

Catherine was thoroughly taken aback. Did he really believe all that garbage? "You must have misinterpreted things. I mean, California is not exactly known for its retiring women. They *couldn't* have been interested only in picking your brain. Not with a body like yours staring them in the face..." His look said it all. He believed it. Either his power of perception was the worst ever, or the two babes he'd run into had been the most myopic in the history of the universe that they hadn't seen what was right in front of their noses—a damn fine specimen of manhood, that's what. "Well. This is simply amazing. Are you saying I can go back to being my usual forthright self? These last few days have been absolute hell. I've never been much good at subtlety. I'll tell you right now, I don't care a whit about your brain.''

"That's very reassuring . . . I think.''

Catherine had to laugh at his perplexed look. "Well, you wanted straightforward. From now on, what you see is what you get.''

"You're so different from anyone I've ever met before. I'm not sure what to make of you. You're like an exotic, brightly colored bird flashing in and out of my consciousness. I can't seem to get a good enough glimpse to see what's really there underneath the bright plumage. But I think I'd like to.''

"You want to do the pursuing? I *have* made you uncomfortable with my directness!'' She'd known it all along. "You want to play the more traditional male role?''

Jay thought about it for a minute. "Maybe subconsciously I'm ill at ease with the roll reversal, but that isn't really what I want, either.'' He posed the query almost plaintively. "Can't we just enjoy the next few days and let things develop however they will?''

Now is was Catherine's turn to take a moment to think. If she really opened herself to him over the next few days, she stood a good chance of being really hurt when he left. On the other hand, at least his plan would provide a *chance* for something to grow between them, as he couldn't very well avoid her under the circumstances. "Okay,'' she managed, slipping her warm hand over the larger, hair-sprinkled one that had again left the steering wheel and taken up a position on her thigh just above her knee. "I'll help you take care of the dynamic trio as much as I can for the next week, and we'll try to enjoy each other's company—that is, if the two concepts aren't mutually exclusive. We'll see what happens.'' She crossed her fingers and sent up a prayer.

He twisted his hand underneath hers, turning his palm up and squeezing hers. "Good. We'll have fun, you'll see."

But Jay was the one who saw. Because of their late although brief nap in the car, nobody was tired when bedtime rolled around. Catherine had helped prepare dinner. She'd held her breath, but the tuna casserole didn't seem to offend any of the tiny palettes. They seemed to find the potato chips generously scrunched over the top a particular delicacy. The green beans didn't sell particularly well, but she and Jay presented a firm front, and there was no ice cream or Oreos until everyone had eaten the required minimum of ten. Emi was most exact in her counting, and Catherine wisely ignored the two Toddy chucked under the table. She was not about to get into a war of wills with that particular child.

They had wrestled on the floor in the living room, Jay appearing to enjoy it as much as the little ones. In between the war whoops, Catherine worried about the plastered ceiling in the apartment below. But not overly. They were having too good a time—and their minds were off their mother.

She washed up in the kitchen while Jay gave them baths. When she went in to pick up the bathroom, she couldn't imagine how such a large tub could be such a failure at holding water. Hollis would have to check it for leaks later. They read numerous bedtime stories, clucking over *The Cat in the Hat* and despairing with the mother of *The Runaway Bunny*. After two glasses of water each, they tucked the little sprites into bed in their respective rooms and each one of the threesome stared up owlishly, not in the least ready for slumber. Fearlessly, Catherine turned out each light and left the rooms, leaving both doors slightly ajar and dragged her flagging body away from the area. If working all day in a physical job like grocery clerking didn't have her in shape for a day or two of playing mommy, she didn't know what would. How did Iris do it?

Jay took her hand and led her into the living room, pulling her down on the couch beside him. "Stay a bit," he urged.

"I really ought to go. I haven't gotten anything done on the apartment today." It was a token protest. She made no move to leave.

"Hollis ought to be home from visiting Iris any minute. Then I'll come help you with whatever needs doing." Catherine looked doubtful, but Jay was persistent. He ran his fingers through her tumbling brown mane, commenting as he did so, "You have the most beautiful hair, Rosie. It lures a man in, urging him closer. Are you sure you don't have any relatives who make their living out at sea calling sailors to their demise?" he asked whimsically.

Catherine giggled and lay her head back against the sofa's overstuffed cushions, trapping Jay's hand. "Now I'm a siren, no less." Her eyes sparkled brightly as she smiled up at him.

Jay brought his other hand up to make up for the loss of the first one, and used it to trace a shivery line along the length of her small jaw, starting from behind one ear. He was just extending the line to reach the opposite matching pink shell and leaning to kiss her trembly lips when a Lilliputian-sized voice piped in, "It's lonely in there. What're you guys doing out here, huh? How come it's so dark? Want me to turn the lights on so you can see, huh?"

Jay's head swiveled and his eyes pinned the half-pint culprit to the wall. He ordered, "Stop, John. Don't turn on the lights. Rosie and I can see just fine. We eat lots of carrots, don't we, Rosie?" Catherine nodded mutely and Jay continued, "What are you doing out of bed?"

"Can't sleep," the small fry replied laconically.

"Of course, you can't sleep. Nobody can sleep standing up," Jay pointed out logically. "That's why you have to stay in bed. That way, when the mood hits, you're already in position."

"Huh?"

"Go back to bed, John. It's late, and your dad's going to be mad at me if he comes home and finds you up."

There was nothing wrong with this child's thought processes. "Why should I be the one to go to bed if you're the one that's going to be in trouble?" Catherine buried her face in her hands in disbelief. *Go away, John,* she silently implored. Things had just been getting interesting.

Jay turned to her and inquired rhetorically, "How old did you say this kid was?"

"I'm four," John replied helpfully. He blinked and advised, "Maybe you and Catherine ought to go to bed. Then Daddy won't be mad."

Jay seemed to like that suggestion, and turned to Catherine for her approval. "What do you say, Rosie? You want to go to bed with me?" There was no response from behind the curtain of her hands and Jay turned back to little John. "I'll discuss it with her, John. For now, you march back into bed and stay put, understand?"

"I need a drink."

"You've just had two."

"I'm still thirsty."

"You're also going to float your bed out. No more drinks. Go back to bed."

"But—"

"No ands, ifs, or buts, either. March, buddy."

The little one's shoulders sagged in defeat, and he turned to retrace his steps down the hall. Catherine and Jay heard the door click shut and turned back to each other.

"Now, as I was saying, you have the most gorgeous thick hair."

Jay had evidently liked the direction things were taking before their interruption.

"And I'm sure I've never seen such black, black eye-lashes—and so long—before in my life."

"They're fake. I glue them on every morning." She was getting nervous. Jay seemed to approach every task with single-minded determination. It looked like she was the task of the moment.

"They're not. I watched you get dressed this morning, remember? You didn't have time for makeup."

"Oh, yeah." She never could tell a convincing story.

But Jay no longer cared about her eyelashes, natural or not. He brought his face forward and buried his nose in her hair. "God, you smell good, Rosie. Your hair smells like warm sunshine. Clean and fresh." He used his mouth to slowly wend a path over the taut skin covering her high, wide cheekbone. "And your skin is so smooth," he muttered as he nibbled. "Mmm, hold still while I try the other side."

"I miss my mommy. Where's my mommy?" Emily hiccuped in front of them between deep sobs. "She's been gone a long, long time, and I want to see her."

Catherine reached out and pulled the miserable bundle at her knees into her lap and crooned softly while cuddling her. "Mommy's sick, baby. Remember I told you she had to stay at the hospital so the doctor can take care of her until she's all better?"

"I'd take care of her," the child returned in such a heart-rending fashion that Catherine's tear glands began to threaten the little makeup she had managed to apply in the Santa's Village restroom.

"Mommy will be home in just a few more days, and she'll still have to have someone take care of her, believe me. You need to go back to bed now and rest up so you can help her out when she comes home."

"But I want her now!"

"I know you do, but we just have to be brave. It's hard, but there's nothing else to be done."

Jay rose from his position on the sofa. "Come on, Emily. I'll tuck you back in, okay?"

Emi hung her head and her long honey-brown hair hid her face. "I didn't get to say my prayers. Mommy always hears our prayers."

Prayers. Of course. How could they have been so stupid? Especially a prayer for poor sick Mommy. Maybe she could donate the prayers she'd said to help herself drift off the previous sleepless evening. Could you backdate Hail Marys?

Jay was obviously feeling equally guilty at this oversight. "We'll take care of that little problem right now. And we'll say a special prayer for Mommy in the hospital that she gets well quick. You go on back to your room. I'll be right there."

As he started for the hallway, Catherine rose and looked around for her purse and apartment keys.

Jay turned back and asked, "You're not leaving, are you? Hang on for just a minute, and I'll be right back."

But Catherine shook her head firmly. "No, Jay. I've got to get going. I want to run out to the Seven-Eleven and pick up some things before I start working on the hallway."

Jay sighed and capitulated gracefully. "Yeah, I guess this isn't working out exactly the way I had hoped. Go ahead and get to work on your project. I'll go to the store when Hollis gets back. It's getting dark, and I don't want you out by yourself."

"I go out by myself all the time," Catherine felt impelled to point out.

"Not while I'm around," Jay retorted firmly. "Just tell me what you need." He looked at her expectantly.

Catherine studied him for a long moment and concluded he was not going to let her out the door unless she promised not to go to the store herself. His whole stance radiated firm opposition and self-righteous purpose.

Brother, he probably thought he'd be picking up cleaning solutions or paintbrushes. Was he in for a surprise. "Oh, all right." This was embarrassing, but he may as well learn her favorite little foible right now. "Get me six packages of Twinkies and drop them off, will you?"

Jay's jaw dropped and his warm brown eyes communicated surprise. "You want six packages of Twinkies?"

"And if you want some, buy an extra package. I don't share my Twinkies."

"Catherine Rose," Jay began disapprovingly, and Catherine noticed how easily the "Rosie" had been dropped as he prepared to voice his disapproval. "Nobody could eat six packages of Twinkies without doing absolutely terrible things to their blood sugar levels." He stared down the length of his impressive nose in what she imagined to be his best professorial manner.

"I'm not going to eat them all at once," she soothed. "I've had a rather trying day, and I don't imagine tomorrow's going to be much better. I swear I'll only have one or two tonight. I'm stockpiling for the future."

"But *Twinkies*?"

"Jay, it's my one and only indulgence. I don't smoke, I seldom swear, and I only drink once a year on New Year's Eve when I have a little eggnog, well—I guess my birthday, too. Now what's a Twinkie or two amidst all that virtue?"

"They're so sweet, though—"

"Sometimes I need a little sugar lift to give me a boost."

"A *little* sugar lift?"

"As I said, a boost."

"But six packages . . . this is so . . . disgusting."

"You're getting repetitive, Jay." Catherine crossed her arms and tapped her toe. "As I told you, I'm perfectly capable of going to the store and buying my own Twinkies, if you can't face the prospect."

He threw up his arms in surrender and rolled his eyes in resignation. "All right. Six packages. I just hope you don't go into a hyperglycemic coma or something on me."

"Not to worry. I ate three packages in one sitting a few days ago, and I'm still around to tell the tale."

"Oh, my God."

"Jay—" Catherine began warningly.

"Rosie—" Jay contraposed. He leaned to place a kiss against her furrowed forehead. "I'm not sure I'm up to handling a Twinkie junkie, but I'll bring them over as soon as I can get out, okay?" He didn't wait for a response before taking her by both shoulders and turning her about. Whacking her lightly on the rump, he directed, "Now go on. Get out of here before I change my mind."

Simultaneously there was a piteous cry from the opposite end of the apartment. "Uncle Juli, I can't find my blankie!"

Catherine got while the getting was good. She heard Jay groan as she went through the kitchen. "What gods have I offended to deserve this?" And then he called louder, "I'll be right there, honey. Do you remember where you saw it last?" His voice faded. "I thought that was too much to ask for—Don't worry, sweetheart, we'll find it."

Catherine shut the door gently behind her and crossed to the tranquil quiet of her own peaceful apartment.

It was ten o'clock before Jay showed up. Catherine waited at the top of the stairs while he dragged himself up the final flight. "I'm beat," he informed her. "Tracking earthquakes is nothing like this."

"Parenthood getting you down, Uncle Juli?" Catherine questioned callously as she took the brown paper sack with her Twinkies away from him.

Jay merely glared.

Catherine slung an arm around his waist—reaching his shoulders was out of the question. "Come on, I'll put the kettle on. Perk you right up."

"Too hot," he objected. "Besides, you'd probably expect me to watch you dunk Twinkies in your tea, wouldn't you?"

"Don't be absurd, a lady never dunks her Twinkies in mixed company, didn't you know?"

Jay was well inside the kitchen by that point. "Hey, what's this? I thought you were going to work on the hall."

Catherine looked down on her project spread all over the kitchen table. "These are for the hall. I thought I'd make a set of wood-block prints of wildflowers native to northern Illinois for the wall in here. If I print them in sepia tones on rice paper and put them in dark-stained frames, it should make a rather effective grouping, don't you think?"

Jay studied the set of six designs Catherine was transferring to wooden blocks in preparation for carving. Their simplicity was deceiving. With just a few lines delineating areas of light and dark, Catherine had caught the essence of each variety, differentiating it from any other.

"Rosie, these are *good*," he said as he studied the Queen Anne's lace she was working on just then. "You could sell these if you wanted to. Why don't you make several prints of each and try?"

"No, they're not that good. Not gallery good, and I haven't got the time for art and craft shows. They're usually on weekends in farflung places with entry fees and things. I have to work every weekend. It's not worth it."

"How do you know they're not gallery good?" Jay queried as he sat opposite her at the kitchen table, watching as she finished using carbon paper to transfer the design onto the woodblock. "An old fraternity brother of mine opened a gallery someplace around here. I could—"

"No!" Jay looked up from watching her hands, surprised by her vehemence. "I mean... I know, that's all. Look, don't you think I've tried to find my niche in geniusness? I'm telling you there just isn't one. I took some of my work around once. The people were kind, but the consensus was pretty much the same. I'm adequate. I even have a certain amount of flair and style, but I'm no Picasso. The world will never hold its collective bated breath waiting for the next series of Escabito prints."

"I can't stand the way you're always putting yourself down, Rosie. You're constantly telling me what a no-talent you are and then turning right around and carving out a beautiful set of wood-block prints, or laying carpeting, or putting just the right dinner on the table to keep three picky kids happy. What is it with you?"

"I do not put myself down," Catherine came back insistently. "You're the one that's being unrealistic. It's taken me a long time to accept myself as I am. To know that while I have lots of minor talents and small gifts, I have no area of genius. Try to understand. I would have sold my soul a few years back for even a small area of genius. In my family tree, an IQ under one hundred and twenty is the equivalent of mental retardation. Heck, one hundred and thirty is marginal."

Jay snorted his disbelief, but Catherine ranted on. "It's true. Anything less than ninety-fifth percentile on those national end of the year tests you take in grammar school and high school and you were d-u-m-b—dumb. The slightly above average groups—the fifth and sixth stanines—where I usually fell, you might as well shoot yourself." She flipped her safety goggles down over her eyes and leaned to plug in her small power drill. "I've finally come to a place where I can live with myself. I couldn't bear it if you tried to build me up into something I'm not. Accept me the way I am or leave me alone, Jay."

Jay leaned forward to watch what she was doing. "Frankly," he said to the top of her shiny brown mop. "I think you're just copping out because the competition was a little bit stiff and you were afraid to make the effort."

Catherine straightened and pushed her protective goggles up on top of her head. "You haven't heard a word I've said, have you?" she accused. "I just finished telling you I tried to market my things and was told I didn't have the talent to make a go of it. And don't lean so close, you'll get a wood chip in your eye. Then you'll really be in trouble." The gentle whir of the drill motor was all that was audible as she again lowered her eyewear and leaned to touch the tool's rotating bit to the block of wood. Instantly the noise level increased, causing Jay to raise his voice as flying bits of wood filled the air.

"Hey!" he protested, flinging his arms protectively over his computer. "You're getting sawdust all over my hardware!"

Catherine didn't even look up from her work. "So get a plastic bag from under the sink and cover it up."

"Oh . . . good idea." Jay seemed surprised by the ease of the solution. Catherine just shook her head as he rose to search out the plastic.

Looking up ten minutes later, Catherine discovered Jay still sitting across from her watching each move she made.

"Don't you have something you wanted to work on?" she questioned. "What about the southern Illinois report?"

"I'm not in the mood." He shrugged his shoulders, never raising his eyes from her rotating drill, fascinated by each cut carved into the wood's surface. "What happens after this?"

"Jay, I can't work with you staring at me. Why don't you go into the hall and see what color we should paint the walls?"

"We?"

"We," Catherine stressed.

Jay shrugged again. "I don't know anything about color."

"I never said I'd actually use your choice."

"You're just trying to get rid of me."

"You're incredibly perceptive."

He was gone for all of three minutes. "White," he announced as he reentered the kitchen work area.

"How exciting," she murmured dryly. "What about the ceiling?"

"Ceilings are always white, too," Jay frowned.

"Not necessarily," she contradicted. "It's true that white is a very expansive choice and probably mandatory in rooms with low ceilings. Otherwise you'd feel like the ceiling was right on top of your head. But that hall is narrow and tall. I'll bet the ceilings in this old building are ten, twelve feet. I was thinking of something light on the walls, like a tapioca to expand the room for as big a feel as we could get and then bring the ceiling down to more human proportions by painting the top foot of the walls and the ceiling a strong caramel." She had sat back in her chair and turned off the drill as she expounded on her decorating ideas. "Toast might be a nice choice, too."

"Catherine, do you hear yourself? Anybody who can—"

"Oh, go home, Jay. I don't want to talk about this anymore."

"Rosie—"

"Jay, go home before I break something over your thick skull. You're out of your field. How can you judge my abilities or lack of same when it's outside your own area of expertise?"

"I know what I like, damn it."

"Wonderful. So do I, and I like you, but not right now." She stood on tiptoe and kissed him on the chin. "Good night. See you tomorrow."

"Count on it, lady," he growled.

"Sleep tight, sweet prince."

Catherine latched the screen door firmly behind his unwilling but nevertheless receding back.

Chapter Six

The temperature had dropped into the low seventies overnight. Catherine stood at her open bedroom window bathing in the delightful offshore breeze being produced courtesy of Lake Michigan. She was grateful for her third-floor apartment that allowed her to leave windows open at night without fear. Any pervert reaching her Rapunzel's lair would be too pooped from the climb to take wicked advantage of her charms.

She propped her elbows on the windowsill, cupping her chin in her hands. The sky was just beginning to lighten in the east and Catherine craned her neck, searching in the predawn dark for a glimpse of the rising sun. At times like this she wished she was able to afford an apartment on the lake a few blocks over. The view of the sun rising in pink and golden splendor out of the dawn-tinted lake was magnificent. Instead she had to wait for morning's clarion to rise high enough to clear the brick three-and four-story buildings that formed her own personal horizon.

She turned away from the window in disappointment. It was always too late. The pinks and golds had given way by then, leaving her nothing but brilliant blue sky studded with puffy white cumulus—and that was available to the any-time riser.

In the bathroom she pasted up the word *unctuous*, even though she already knew its meaning, and proceeded to the kitchen. She had thrown out *triskaidekaphobia*. She didn't know anybody afraid of the number thirteen and didn't care to. Neither did she want to appear too picky, so the next word in the box, *unctuous*, got the honors.

Throwing open the back door for the morning breeze, she heard Jay and wondered if he was a natural early riser. She smirked a little smirk. From what she could catch, Jay was deep in a one-sided discussion with Toddy on why he should let go of the cereal box and wait until Uncle Juli was through disposing of his overnight diaper and sodden pj's at which point Uncle Juli would pour the cereal into a bowl instead of sprinkling it all over the floor. From the sound of it, Jay was losing the debate. She laughed outright as she shame-lessly eavesdropped on his, "Emily, I know you're a big girl now, but I'd rather do it myself. Just give me a minute." This was followed by a sternly delivered, "Toddy, I said *No!*" and the grating wail of Tod's thin voice. She wondered how long it would be before Jay came running for rescue. She was determined to get as much done as possible before he called for reinforcements.

Washing and preparing the hall walls took her until the posted early opening hour of the paint store she patron-ized. She was back, using a miter box to cut trim for the caramel-color demarkation line when the knocking began at her back door.

"How much longer are you going to be?" Jay demanded with absolutely no preamble.

"Well, I had a little trouble sleeping last night. The air was so humid, you know. So I'm a little tired, but other than that, I'm fine. And how are you?" she responded as she unlatched and kicked open the screen door.

"Don't be cute. You're looking at a desperate man. Far too desperate to appreciate any attempts at humor." There was a resounding crash from the apartment next door and Jay paled, muttering dark imprecations under his breath as he yelled, "What's going on over there? You're supposed to be watching TV. Behave yourselves for just a minute!"

Catherine couldn't prevent a laugh from escaping. She hastily clamped her lips shut when Jay shot her a fulminating look from beneath impressively furrowed brows. "I'm going to put on the first coat of paint before I come," she advised before he could get in the first salvo. He paled further. She quickly assured, "It shouldn't take too long. An hour or two at most. Promise." She raised her fingers in the old Girl Scout pledge sign, but Jay was too busy calculating the seriousness of a further crash to notice.

He nodded when Catherine queried, "Are they dressed yet? Then take them to the park and get them out of the apartment. That's what Iris does. They can race around to their heart's content and be good and tired for their naps."

The thought of the children's nap time seemed to boost Jay's spirits and he left, temporarily girded for further battle.

It was twelve o'clock on the nose when Catherine reached to roll up the spattered dropcloth she had used to protect her new hall carpeting. She knew because the Angelus was ringing from the spire of St. Nick's, a few blocks away. She also knew because Jay and his charges could be heard noisily tromping up the back stairs.

"Ow! He's pinchin' me again, Uncle Juli!"

"John, if you do that one more time, I'm going to swat your bottom, understand? Emily, it couldn't have hurt that badly. Stop shrieking, the baby's starting to cry. Shhh, Toddy. It's all right."

"It did so hurt a whole lot. He only pinched a teensy tiny bit of skin. That hurts a whole lot more than a big piece, you know."

"I'm sure it does, Emi. But be brave, will you? If Tod starts screaming while I'm holding him, my eardrum may never recover. It may be permanently damaged from last time already."

"Well, you gotta hold John still so I can pinch him back."

"Lord save me from retributive females."

Catherine met them on the rear landing. "Bad day at Black Rock?" she inquired brightly.

Jay rolled his eyes comically for her benefit and fumbled one-handed in his pockets to retrieve a giant ring of keys. Catherine watched him awkwardly working with them for a moment before relieving him of their weight. "What do you need all these keys for?" she questioned before commenting, "You look like a jail warden. It's this skeleton key, isn't it?" She inserted the heavy metal key into the appropriate slot, turned the knob and swung the door open without waiting for him to respond.

Jay stepped back, sweeping his free hand before him. "After you, madam." Emily giggled and stepped into the kitchen. When John would have followed, Jay held him back to grab Catherine's arm as she turned for her own rear door. "You, too, my dear. This way." And he kept a death grip on her arm as though afraid she would try to slip away.

And he was right in his thinking, Catherine acknowledged to herself. She would have. "Let me clean up," she urged, tugging ineffectually against his iron hold. That kind of strength hadn't developed sitting behind a desk all day. It made her wonder just exactly how he had acquired it.

"Where is your sense of charity?" the object of her thoughts demanded. "Who's your minister? He has failed dismally in his duties and I intend to tell him so."

Laughing, Catherine protested, "Just give me time to wash my face and hands, then I'll come help. I promise."

"There's a sink right here. Running water and everything. No need to go home whatsoever." And he pulled Catherine into the small apartment, kicking the door shut behind him as though to block her escape route.

"All right, all right," Catherine surrendered, inhaling his heady male scent appreciatively as he passed on her way to the sink tap. As she bathed up to her elbows, she queried, "So what's on the menu? P.B. and J.? B.L. and T.?"

"I never gave a thought to *what* I was going to give them for lunch," Jay admitted with a blank look. "Just the fact that I was going to have to give it to them." His voice took on the now familiar note of panic. "I hope to God there's some food in the house." He looked around the room as though seeing the fingerprint-proof finished refrigerator and kitchen cabinets with their hidden stores of food for the first time. "What'll we do if there's nothing here?" he asked a little desperately.

"Go to the store," she answered pragmatically as she opened a cabinet door to peer inside.

"Oh, God," he muttered. "They'll be beside themselves by then. They've been whining for the last twenty minutes." He ran a hand distractedly through his hair, leaving it endearingly rumpled. Catherine's hand itched to do the same. "That's why we left the park. John has been taking little pinches of Emi and pretending to eat her. That's when I thought to check the time. It's after twelve now."

"Jay, a few more minutes one way or the other isn't going to make that big of a difference. Do they look on the verge of collapse to you? Now stop worrying and help me look. We'll find something." She pulled a loaf of whole-wheat bread and a three-quarter's empty bag of Cheetos out from behind a giant-sized container of oatmeal and set them on the counter.

They found several individually wrapped slices of American cheese, part of a stick of margarine, and three apples in the refrigerator. There was a lone banana on top of it. Catherine made grilled cheese while Jay helped the small fry wash up. She felt warm and happy inside herself to be working next to Jay. She let John divide the pitifully few Cheetos into piles. In an effort to keep him honest, Emi and Toddy got to choose their piles first.

After lunch Jay again washed them up while Catherine cleaned the kitchen. And although Emi protested she was too big for a nap, she was agreeable to a quiet time in bed with a book. Jay and Catherine both exhaled on a sigh of relief when they were finally able to close the bedroom doors behind them and retreat to the brightly decorated living room. Actually it was a bit too intense for Catherine's taste. The paint on the full-tone, egg-yoke-yellow walls had been carefully chosen to match a sprig in the bright floral fabric covering the couch, and it did. But it was painfully... bright. Catherine blinked, as she always did when entering Iris's living room in the daylight. On the walls were four pictures of orange flowerpots, two with jonquils, two with mums silkscreened onto framed mirrors. The sun glinted off the reflective surface and Catherine squinted as it hit her full in the face. "Wow!" she mumbled as she shaded her eyes with a hand and practically felt her way across the room with the other.

"What's the matter?" Jay inquired, squinting himself as he watched her grope across the room.

"Let's sit in the kitchen. I know it's yellow, too, but this room is downright painful when the sun is up."

Jay looked around him, surprised. "Is that why I get a headache sitting in here? The color?"

Catherine nodded. "That, plus all the mirrors. You have to be careful when you're decorating. There's a whole psychological theory built around the moods that can be created by choices in color. And, of course, it works in the reverse. You can tell a lot about the state of a person's psyche by the palette they choose to work with in their home."

Jay sat with a sigh of relief on a yellow plastic-cushioned kitchen chair and looked at her a little oddly. "How do you know all that?"

She shrugged and lowered herself into the chair next to his. The backs of her thighs stuck uncomfortably to the plastic in the humidity. Leaning her elbows on the Formica tabletop, she responded, "I read it somewhere." Jay looked ready to pursue that line of conversation, but Catherine headed it off. "Don't start, Jay. It's called being well-rounded. Nothing more. You narrow-minded geniuses wouldn't understand." Jay seemed unconvinced but left it.

They waited for the sun to shift before Catherine dusted and vacuumed in the living room. She also scrubbed the bathroom, figuring it would be unwise to press Jay too hard in this, his first encounter with real-world living. She didn't want him deciding it wasn't worth pursuing!

Jay seemed to realize his small nap-time hiatus was almost over and the tick in his eye picked up tempo as he turned to say, "Do you think you could make some chocolate-chip cookies or something for when they wake up?"

"It's too hot to heat up the kitchen baking, Jay."

"But what will I do with them when they wake up? Do you have anything at your place I could give them with milk after their nap?"

Catherine frowned at the vacuum cleaner before responding. It seemed to have grown and refused to squeeze the final inch necessary for her to close the closet door on it. Giving it one last shove, she quickly pushed the door shut and nodded in satisfaction as she heard the door catch. "Don't open that," she directed. "It'll be like Fibber McGee's closet. Everything in it will rain down on your head." She pivoted away from the closet and started to walk away.

"Rosie," Jay wailed as he followed in hot pursuit. "Think of something!"

"Calm down. I'm just going to check out the cabinets one more time. It seems to me I saw some Rice Krispies out there. Take it easy. Your eye is starting to go bonkers again."

Jay threw up his hands and spoke to the heavens. "'Take it easy,' she says," he uttered in despair. "She's giving them breakfast cereal for an afternoon snack and I'm to take it easy. Rosie, nobody eats cereal at two-thirty in the afternoon, for crying out loud. Are you sure it's too hot to bake?"

Catherine ignored him. "Ahh," she said. "Here's what I was looking for." She peered inside and exclaimed. "Good. Plenty left, too." With that she stooped to examine the insides of a lower cabinet and pulled out a saucepan. She plopped it on a burner, lobbed half a stick of margarine retrieved from the refrigerator into the pan and clicked on the flame.

Finally she handed a long-handled wooden spoon to Jay and flicked her hair behind her shoulders with a shake of her head. "Here," she said. "Don't let that burn. I'll be right back."

"Rosie! You can't leave. Where are you going?" he asked, looking prepared to bodily block the kitchen doorway if necessary.

"Have a little faith, Jay. I said I'd be right back. I need some things from my place. Unless you cleaned me out when you were working over there, we'll be okay."

"Okay how?" Jay questioned a little hysterically. "Rosie, you come back here!" But he spoke to thin air as she had already left. Nervously he turned back to the saucepan, chiding the pot and waving the wooden spoon in a threatening manner. "I hope what they say about watched pots is true, because I haven't the foggiest idea what to do if you start scorching. So don't do anything we'll both regret." Anxiously he watched as the margarine started melting and sizzling around the edges in an ominous manner.

But true to her word, Catherine was back within moments. Taking the spoon from Jay's clammy grasp, she stirred most of a bag of miniature white marshmallows into the pan, coating them with the melted margarine and watching in satisfaction as they began to loose shape and melt into a sticky glop. "Personally, I've never had much use for chocolate-chip cookies," she said conversationally, as if there had been no gap in their speech. "They have no raison d'être. I can't think of a single thing that's good for you in them. I forgot to butter a pan. Fish out a nine-by-thirteen and grease it up for me, will you?"

"Unlike Twinkies," Jay snorted in disbelief as he squatted in front of the lower cabinet to root through its contents. "Now there's a food with real nutritional value. Is this what you want?" He held up a pan for her inspection.

"That's a square, Jay," she pointed out kindly. "It couldn't possibly be nine by thirteen."

"Right," he grunted, turning back to the cabinetful of pans. "I knew that."

"Twinkies," she reminded him, "are my only vice. But Rice Krispie treats have enriched grain and the kids are getting some vitamins out of it...I think." She reached for the cereal box and frowned over its small print.

"Okay, here it is. Now what do you want me to do with it?" Jay rose from the floor, flaunting a rectangular aluminum pan and sniffing the air appreciatively. "Smells good."

"And we didn't appreciably heat up the kitchen," Catherine returned smoothly and gave up reading the box's side panel to begin tipping its contents into the saucepan instead. "Hurry up," she directed. "I'm going to need that in a second."

"You still haven't explained what I'm supposed to do here."

"For heaven's sake, just take a pat of margarine and rub it around in there so this goo doesn't stick to the pan."

Jay looked at the pan and then at the strings of marshmallow hanging from Catherine's spoon. "Okay. I can handle this."

"One can only hope."

He sighed. "It'll be good to get back to California, I can tell you. Back on firm ground. I know what I'm doing there, and I'm good at it." He looked around himself with a wry grin of self-disparagement. "Here I'm always slightly off balance."

Catherine's heart sank at his professed eagerness to leave, but she only responded, "Is that a joke?"

Handing her the greased pan, he looked at her, plainly puzzled. "Is what a joke?"

Shrugging as she spooned the sticky mass into his greased pan, she kept her eyes resolutely on what she was doing.

"That bit about getting back on firm ground. I thought maybe you were being funny."

"What's so funny about that particular figure of speech?" he asked, leaning closer to watch her pat the mixture down firmly into the pan and inhaling her delightful feminine fragrance at the same time.

"Oh, you know—a seismologist, and one who lives on top of the San Andreas fault at that, wanting to get back onto firm ground?"

He looked at her blankly for a moment, then the corners of his eyes began to crinkle and he laughed out loud. "That's good," he chuckled. "And I can't even take credit for it. You're quick. Quicker than I am." His arms encircled her, hugging her back against his massive strength.

Jay casually rested his chin on the top of her shining hair and breathed deeply. He laughed as tiny wisps, grown recalcitrant and wild in the humidity, tickled his nose. Catherine was caught in a quandary, her hands sticky with marshmallow, pot in one and gooey spoon in the other, as Jay let his large hands migrate, one from her waist and one from her shoulders to the beckoning middle ground. She shivered as her thin cotton T-shirt offered no protection from the marauding invaders. Squirming was useless, she soon discovered. It only increased the sensations that had her nerve endings standing on end.

Setting the pan down, she carefully placed the spoon into its confines before ordering in frustration, "Jay, stop that." She didn't really expect him to, and he didn't. She contemplated her hands. They were free of the pot and spoon now, but bits of candy-coated Rice Krispies clung tenaciously to her fingertips. Her breath came faster. "You're not playing fair," she complained. "My hands are all stuck up and I can't retaliate."

His head lowered, and he spoke two syllables. "I know."
His thumbs began a slow-motion massage, rubbing back
and forth across her sensitive nipples, making her gasp. In
her braless state, the sensations he evoked were unbearably
sensuous. Her breath picked up pace.

In desperation she twisted in his arms, turning a full one
hundred and eighty degrees. Facing him now, she stuck a
fingertip into her mouth intending to lick it clean. Catherine
watched Jay's face as she sucked, hoping for an early
warning of a further attack on her senses.

Jay smiled easily down on her wary features, his eye
hardly bothering him at all. He loosened one arm, but there
was no escape yet. A man of Jay's size and strength—and
magnetism—didn't require more than one hand to anchor
her solidly. Arching her upper body away from him was
impossible without the use of both hands to prop against his
chest. She let her breath whoosh out between gently parted
lips as Jay took her left hand, still sticky with melted
marshmallow and cereal bits and popped her index finger
into his mouth, sensually sucking it free of candy residue
before moving on to the next, all the while never breaking
eye contact.

Catherine watched him without blinking. She swallowed
hard. Could this man, responsible for leaving her panting
with slightly open mouth and flushed face, be the same endearingly
awkward giant of a few days ago? How was it
possible for this man, who couldn't grease a pan without
direction, to turn her bones into mush in just a few short
moments? And she *was* melting. Soon the arm clamping her
to him would be a necessity, not to keep her from escaping,
but as a support to keep her from dissolving into a gelatinous,
shimmering puddle at his feet.

What she would do if Jay ever decided to take advantage
of her weakness for him when they were totally alone,

Catherine couldn't begin to imagine. But once again, noise from the back half of the apartment saved her and brought an abrupt halt to their love play. Newton's triple proof of self-sustaining perpetual motion was awake.

Catherine rocked on the balls of her feet as she squatted by the old-fashioned tub and reached to squeeze a wash-cloth full of water down Toddy's rounded little tummy. A sigh of relief escaped her pursed lips as the end of the last bath came into sight. Bedtime for three little munchkins would quickly follow. The kids were darling, far better than most she came in contact with at the grocery store, but she honestly didn't know where Iris found the energy to deal with them on a fourteen-hour-a-day, day-in day-out basis.

The afternoon had gone quite well, all things considered. The kids had been familiar with Rice Krispie treats and for-tunately required nothing disgusting to enhance their flavor like the ketchup on the eggs. Taking them to Evanston's lighthouse beach for the remainder of the afternoon had been an inspiration. It wasn't far from the apartment building, and when the rolling navy lake water and the sand-drip castles she had taught them to build on the shore failed to hold their attention, they had climbed the spiraling light-house stairs—"eight gazillion feet up into the sky" accord-ing to Emi—to investigate the huge beacon perched in its glass-enclosed dome. The caretaker had his spiel down pat and the children had been duly impressed.

Catherine, unfortunately, hadn't heard a word, she re-membered ruefully as she finished rinsing Tod, wrapped him in a towel and handed him to Jay for the pajama-ing pro-cess. They had formed a rather credible assembly-line-type operation with Jay undresssing them, handing them over to Catherine for bathing, and then taking them back to finish things up. The amount of sand left in the bottom of the tub was incredible. Catherine eyed it disbelievingly before trying to swish it down the drain with her washcloth.

Her eyes took on a languid dreamy look—the blue of the lake on a calm, warm day with no wind. Her efficient moves to wipe down the tub became haphazard and ineffectual, missing large areas of glistening sand, as she thought of what *had* held her attention in place of the caretaker's informative talk.

Jay, in a bathing suit, was lethal. He should have been arrested. It wasn't that his suit was one of those male racing numbers that leave nothing to the imagination. Far from it. It had been rumpled, loose, and white with two navy stripes down each side and a bare one-inch slit at the sides. No, Jay didn't flaunt it. He didn't have to.

She had always known Jay had been blessed with broad shoulders, the kind every woman dreams of leaning on. But that intellectual knowledge had not prepared her for the physical reality. Broad was an understatement of the first order. They were wide and brawny and went on and on. Generously overlayed with finely carved sinew and muscle, they were veneered with a liberal furring that began with an arbitrary line at the base of his neck decided upon by his razor and tapering down the rolling contoured chest and flatly planed stomach to the elasticized waistband of his suit. This was no body by Atlas, but a leanly conditioned strength Catherine found far more appealing than that bicep-built-upon-bicep look bodybuilders worked so hard to achieve.

Catherine lowered herself into the nursery rocker, prepared to read Emi her choice of stories while Jay finished diapering Tod. She watched Jay out of the corner of her eye as she hoisted the little girl onto her lap and adjusted her position there. His shirt was back on, but had been left unbuttoned in a casual sort of way. He was barefoot and in dry sport shorts that left long broadly muscled legs visible for her perusal. As he moved about tickling and dressing the baby, the open shirt gapped from his chest, giving Catherine tantalizing glimpses of the short reddish brown hair to be found there.

She shook her head to clear it. How could this man be so awkward and unsure of himself? And yet she knew it wasn't put on. She had seen the looks the other women on the beach had given him. She had been shocked. After all, they were obviously married. Young mothers with small children. But as she had studied the object of their fascination, she realized they'd have to be dead and cold to the touch not to react to the all male, overscale form that had dropped so precipitously into their sandy midst.

The funny thing was, Jay had been oblivious to their intimate perusals. Either he was terrifically near-sighted and/or oblivious to the world around him, or the kids and she were a lot more scintillating and fascinating than she gave them credit for being. She had come away convinced that the man honestly didn't know he had caused a furor there on the beach. Incredible. But not so bad from where she sat. After all, the sneak attacks he had initiated on her body of late bespoke a certain burgeoning interest in her. Now if she could just capitalize on that before he became too aware of his incredible appeal. The knuckle-brain evidently believed that his small, inconsequential muscle tick negated all of that heavy-duty sex appeal he had been blessed with. It was . . . incredible.

Chapter Seven

The telephone began to ring two pages into *Bedtime for Teddy*. Jay answered it in the kitchen, but the connection must have been poor. He was yelling into the phone and Catherine eavesdropped shamelessly.

"Can you hear me now, Susan? My God, I'll wake up half the neighborhood at this rate."

Susan? And just who was Susan? Catherine shifted Emi's position on her lap and read, "'It was time for Teddy to go to bed.'"

"Actually, things are in a bit of a muddle here. Yes. My brother and his wife are in the middle of a family crisis, and I'm watching the kids."

He was watching the kids? What was Catherine doing, organizing books of green stamps? "'The shadow that lived under the big oak tree in Teddy's yard had grown all afternoon until it had stretched as far as the rabbit hole where Teddy lived.'"

"—not going to be able to get away just yet. Sorry, I guess it'll fall to you. You're worth two of anyone else anyway. This'll just prove it."

Well, to heck with him! Shy and retiring, my foot. What a con artist. Playing on her sympathies when all the time... " 'It was time for Teddy to go to bed.' "

"I thought you weren't going to that conference. Can't stay away from me, huh?"

A small voice piped in, "What's the matter, Catherine? How come you're not turning the page?"

"What? Oh, sorry, darling. Here we go. 'The sun had held itself up in the sky for a long time. Longer than Teddy ever could have, but finally it couldn't hold itself up any more and it fell, landing somewhere behind Farmer Marc's barn.' " *What a bum. She'd like to drop* him *behind Farmer Marc's barn.*

"Can you let Jack know I'll be late getting out to the dig? Great. I was going to ask you to mail me some things, but if you're coming this way anyhow, would you bring out the paperwork stacked on my desk? I'll take you out to dinner."

Catherine pictured the main course. Head of Julius.

Teddy bunny had better get himself safely tucked into bed—and pronto. There was a storm brewing, and while its center wasn't in Farmer Marc's barnyard, its fury would probably wash over everyone and everything in Iris's apartment.

" 'It was time for Teddy to go to bed.' " Catherine practically spat the words out.

"You know me too well."

Did she indeed? " 'Farmer Marc had been in the field all day trying to tame the big tractor that growled and threw dirt and dust at him. But now Farmer Marc had given up and was washing his face—in the very same water the horses drank from—and was going in the farmhouse for his dinner.'"

Jay's warm laugh filtered through the apartment. "I said I'd take you out. Besides that last dinner I made wasn't all *that* bad."

"'It was time for Teddy to go to bed . . . and so he did.'" Catherine snapped the book shut, probably bouncing Teddy right back out of his burrow in the process. "And it's time for all of you to go to bed, too."

"Rosie!" Jay called from the kitchen, evidently done with his phone call. "I can hear your phone ringing. Want me to run over and catch it?"

She shouted back, "Don't bother. Whoever it is will call back." Then she turned to the kids. "Nobody has to go, huh? Okay, then. Everybody into the sack. I'll cover you up and Uncle Juli will come in for good-night hugs and kisses. Jay?" she called.

But there was no response. "Jay?" she tried again. Still nothing. She was just going to investigate when the kitchen door slapped gently shut and footsteps resounded on the linoleum kitchen floor. She met him in the hall.

He had apparently disregarded her advice to ignore the phone, for he greeted her with, "It was some guy named Tony who wanted you to go make gravestone rubbings with him tomorrow after work. Kind of a strange hobby, isn't it? What's he do with the rubbings? I told him you were busy."

Catherine placed her hands on her hips and glared up at him. Her toe tapped in a rhythm Jay would have done well to be wary of. "You told him *what*?"

Jay left his hand on the doorknob to the children's room as he turned and questioned anxiously, "Well, you are going to come help me after work, aren't you? I mean, they won't eat anything I fix them. I just assumed—"

"Don't give me that little-boy-lost bit, Jay. It won't wash. I heard you on the phone just now. You're not the poor lost lamb unsure of his place in the flock and leery of all the ewes that you pretend to be."

Jay blinked twice. "What are you talking about, Rosie?"

"Oh, come off it, Jay," she returned impatiently. "I'm talking about sweet Sue and your dinner plans."

"What about them?" But her expression told him. "You're jealous of *Susan*?" he asked as though he found the idea preposterous.

"Of course not," she prevaricated staunchly. "I think you've been playing on my sympathies, that's all."

"Rosie, Sue's a friend. A co-worker from the institute," he explained. "She's got a mind like a steel trap. I don't think of her like that."

He respected her for her mind. Right. And he could lust after Catherine because she didn't have one. She opened her mouth to give her opinion of that, only to realize he was already gone, having slipped into the nursery moments before.

Catherine watched as Jay delivered goodnight kisses to both bedrooms occupants. He made a show of adjusting the lightweight covers before making his way out to the hall. "Nobody get out of bed now. I'm letting invisible snakes out in the hallway, and I'm sure they'd love to nibble on a little one's toe or two."

"Jay!" Catherine reproved as he closed the door behind him. She was appalled by the innocent look he turned on her. "What a perfectly terrible thing to say! They'll all have nightmares."

Jay shrugged. "Hey, you want to stay here and handle the next hour while they do their jack-in-the-box popping out of bed for drinks, potty, kisses, and forgotten-remembrances-in-their-prayers routine? I had to grow up with invisible snapping alligators, and they were in the bedroom as well as the hall. One toe over the edge of the bed, and you were a goner. That's a lot more vicious than a couple of lousy snakes. Besides, Hollis'll be home from the hospital soon and he can gather them back up. It's the price he pays for hiring cheap labor."

"If they could afford a professional sitter, I'm sure they wouldn't be living in a third-floor walk-up," Catherine scolded as they made their way down the hall.

Jay shrugged again. "I'm sure it won't be the first time Hollis discovers there's no such thing as a free lunch. By the way," he continued as they reached the living room, more useable now that the only light was a low-watt bulb further muted by a heavily pleated lampshade. He pulled her down on the sofa cushion with the bad spring and she slid into his waiting arms. "You had two phone calls while I was at your place. Say, this is nice, isn't it? I could get used to snuggling with a warm woman like this."

A warm woman? Any warm woman? She'd forgotten about the lovely Susan for a minute. Struggling to sit up, she gave Jay an inadvertent poke in the ribs.

"Ouch! Hey, will you relax? I'm not going to pounce—yet." He didn't let her go, and Catherine lay stiffly in his arms. He tangled his large blunt fingers in her rich brown hair, lifting it away from her head to inspect the shiny mass. "Anyway, right after I got rid of that Tony," he frowned in memory of the other man's nerve and asked in an aside, "You got any more like him tucked away? Weird man. I hope you haven't encouraged him by actually helping him make those rubbings before."

"Jay, lots of people make rubbings of tombstones. It's not all that uncommon of a hobby. The older stones can be quite unusual and sometimes are very artistically done."

"Well, don't you do it. It's not for you."

Catherine didn't know if she should cheer or take offense that he felt qualified to lay down rules. "The other phone call?" she prompted.

"Oh, yeah. A Mary Ellen. Said to tell you she's back from her dental convention in Denver and picked up some tokens for your collection and wants you to call her." He looked down to where her head rested on his massive chest and cocked an eyebrow. "So one of your friends is married to a dentist, huh?"

"No, Mary Ellen's the dentist. Her husband teaches second grade."

"Oh." Jay looked nonplussed. "Uh, you collect bus tokens? My mother collects bells, and I've heard of women who collect spoons or thimbles. But bus tokens is a new one on me. You and your friends certainly have some... interesting hobbies. Do you have very many? What does one do with... old bus tokens? I have a collection of coins," he mused thoughtfully as he twined his hand further into her hair. "They're a good investment. But I don't keep them at the house. They're in a bank vault box. A fellow who knows what he's doing calls me every now and then when he sees something interesting. I hardly ever see them."

"That's terrible!" Catherine protested, appalled. "Hobbies are supposed to be fun! Coin collecting can be a good time, but not the way you do it. You're right, that's an investment, not a hobby. How can you stand not to even see them?"

Jay looked down mildly into her clearly askance features. "My question stands. Why would anybody collect bus tokens?"

"Because it's fun! No other reason. And, uh, I don't exactly collect bus tokens, you know."

Again Jay looked down. Now Catherine was the uncomfortable one. "What do you collect, then? What other kinds of tokens are there?"

"Bawdy house tokens?" she whispered in a small voice, not quite looking at him.

Jay's eyes widened in amazement. "I beg your pardon?"

"You heard me." Catherine was finding the short brown hairs curling up the length of Jay's forearm suddenly quite fascinating.

He pulled his arm away as she inadvertently tugged a bit too hard. "Are you talking bawdy house, as in houses of prostitution?" At Catherine's meek nod he exploded, "What the hell kind of tokens do they give? And why the devil would anybody collect them? You know, the more I get to know you, the less I understand you. Rosie, tell me you've never—"

Catherine turned in his arms, propped her forearms on his great chest and gazed up. She could actually feel the air rumbling through his chest cavity in his agitation. "Of course I don't frequent houses of prostitution, Jay. I'm the wrong sex to be buying tokens, for one thing."

"The more I get to know you, the more I think a mere detail like that would not be allowed to stand in your way."

"Now calm down," Catherine cajoled, running an inquisitive finger over his full lower lip. She had completely forgotten Susan for the time being. "It's not *that* unusual a hobby."

"Rosie, *stamps* are a typical thing to collect. Paperweights. Little teacups and saucers, for God's sake. But *bawdy house tokens*? Come on! You can't be serious."

Catherine was beginning to lose her patience. She accepted him the way he was, didn't she? Why did he find it necessary to constantly try to straighten her out? Wasn't he

at all interested in a little lightweight necking, for heaven's
sake? Did he have to keep harping on a perfectly innocent,
insignificant detail of her personality? "Bawdy house tokens are very historical," she began in defense of her hobby
and punched Jay in the chest when he snorted in disbelief.
Great. She'd hurt her hand. "They are! They're first mentioned in ancient Greek history. Epicurius, I believe. They
were brought to New England by the Bulgarians in the sev-
enteenth century and migrated west from there. It was a way
for the house to ensure that the girls weren't cheating by not
turning in the full amount of money paid by the men. This
way, the patrons purchased the tokens downstairs before
even entering the girls' rooms. All the girls had to do was
return the tokens to the madam at the end of the night for a
head count, so to speak."

"I don't believe this."

"I have some great ones," Catherine enthused. "Some of
the more popular girls had their names stamped on them."

"What the hell is wrong with spoons? Susan collects these
little spoons..."

Ah. The lovely Susan again. She would collect something insipid like spoons. Reason enough not to take it up
herself. Catherine wanted as few similarities as possible between the two of them. Lord, what if there were more than
just the two of them? She hadn't thought of that. Women
probably fell like bricks for his bird-with-a-clipped-wing
routine. She became grimly determined to differentiate
herself from the pack. "I've got one for a certain Velvet Ass
Rose, and Big Minnie, who advertises herself as 'one-eighth
ton of quivering delight.' Can't you just picture it? What a
mental image. But my all-time favorite is from Ruth Ja-
cobs's Silver Dollar Hotel in Denver that's marked 'good for
one screw.' Nothing like laying it on the line."

Jay seemed a little glassy-eyed as he looked at her in disbelief.

Catherine wasn't blind. She pointed an accusatory finger up at him. "The trouble with you is that you're too staid and conservative. Nothing can be just for the hell of it. There has to be some underlying worth to excuse its existence or Mr. Propriety here won't have anything to do with it. Coin collecting. Pah!" She flicked her finger in a dismissive gesture. "It shows a decided lack of creativity. I'll bet you decide what to buy by its weight and carat content and don't have anything historically interesting at all. Krugerrands instead of Indian wampum, I'll bet." The way his eye tick picked up speed and the dull flush that crept up his neck told her she was right on target.

"You have no imagination," she decreed. "I could get you started on an antique false eye collection. Now there's a *hobby*. I have this friend who collects them. He may have some duplicates."

"Rosie, I don't want to hear this." He shifted uncomfortably under her weight.

"Sure you do." She dismissed his qualms. "This is good stuff. For example, did you know that in nineteenth century England, if a lady lost her eye, she invariably ordered a blue replacement, no matter what color her other eye was?"

"Uh, no. I didn't know that."

"Well, it's true. It seems Queen Victoria had blue eyes, and they all wanted to emulate her. Fascinating, huh?"

"Fascinating," he returned, looking a little pale. "Listen, couldn't—"

"And then, do you remember that nursery song 'Pop Goes the Weasel'?" Jay nodded reluctantly. It went against his better judgment to encourage her. "They're not referring to an animal in that song." She paused significantly, waiting for his curiosity to get the better of him.

He gave in. "Aren't they?"

"No. A weasel was anything easily pawned when you needed cash in a hurry. False eyes were one of the most popular weasels around."

"Oh, my God." He was no longer pale. He was green.

"What do you think about that?"

"I'm trying hard not to," he groaned. "It's a fairly disgusting concept, if you ask me."

"Mmm, not really. Only sometimes, like when Jack's display case gets bumped and all the eyes look in different directions. That gets hard to handle."

"Aw, Rosie!" It was a cry of despair.

"Okay, okay. Here, you'll like this better. I've got another friend who—"

But Jay had reached his limit. He pulled her close. His mouth hovered over hers. "That's enough of that," he ordered firmly.

She could smell dinner's grand finale—mint chocolate-chip ice cream—on his breath and knew he'd taste like dessert.

"I've got better things on my mind besides your flaky friend's hobbies."

She thought those "other things" sounded a lot more interesting herself, but felt duty bound to defend her friends. "How can you sit there and call my friends flaky? You've never even met them." She had him there. He just didn't seem to care.

He placed one large hand firmly at the back of her head and drew it down, drowning out any further comments with a kiss so fiery, Catherine felt consumed in the conflagration.

In the short time Catherine had know him, Jay's kisses had grown in potency. There was no fumbling, no tentative bumbling. This was pure masculine assuredness, confident in its ability to please, and it did. He drew back momentarily to study her face. There was not a trace of humor lurking in his heated gaze. "My God," he muttered, his breath gusting cleanly against the smooth skin of her cheek. "What you do to me. Any thought other than of you flies right out the window when I'm around you..."

His words trailed off as his lips closed on hers once more in a fierce display designed to show her without further vocal description.

"Jay," she moaned. "Oh, Jay. I can't catch my breath."

"Don't bother," he shot back fiercely. "We'll make up for it later when we're lying awake all alone in our beds." Chills rippled down her back, making her shudder. For now it was skin against skin as he acquired the boldness to slip a hand up under her shirt and directly cup a swelling breast for the first time. Shamelessly she allowed him to draw her bright green T-shirt up and her breath caught as she watched the flames growing in his passion-filled eyes.

He stared. God, he loved it. Finally he raised his eyes unwillingly from her breasts to look, mesmerized, into her face, but those beautiful breasts called him back. Slowly, as if it were a sacred moment, he brought his lips to the trembling crests, gently kissing each one, fascinated by the way they puckered and hardened under his ministration.

Impatiently he pulled the shirt up and over her head, mussing her thick mane of hair and leaving it tousled and swirling heavily around her small shoulders. Again he came to a complete standstill as his gaze locked onto the vision before her. Slowly, so slowly she began to quiver in anticipation, his head began to lower toward the trembling pink tips beneath him.

At first he did nothing but drop random, stinging kisses across the exposed hills and valleys of her chest. "You have the most beautiful breasts I've ever seen," he whispered reverently in the twilighted room.

Catherine was beyond anything but a gasped, "My turn. I want to see you, Jay." Her hands reached to tug the open shirt away from his broad shoulders. She had it pulled almost free when his mouth honed in on the sensitive peak of her breast. Her hands dropped to her side, the shirt left hanging from his waist, caught in his pants. He gained courage, flicking his thumb across one nipple while stabbing at the other with his bold tongue. Jay stopped only long enough to rip his shirt free. Catherine's hands played the length of his spine, running up and down his back, her fingers defining each vertebra in turn. She pressed herself tightly against him.

But the telephone was not yet done for the night. As low as its volume was turned, its muted ring still sounded harsh in the quiet of the apartment and Jay swore at its untimely interruption.

"Damn it. Who the devil can that be? We've already talked to everyone in the continental United States. Stay right here," he instructed. "I'll be right back." He moved toward the telephone and picked it up.

"Mom! Good to hear your voice."

His words seemed slightly uneven but sincere. Yet, from what Iris had said... Catherine sat up and slipped her T-shirt back over her head. It would have taken more brazenness than she possessed to wantonly recline in little more than God's own, listening in while Jay spoke to his mother, the indomitable dragonness figuring so predominantly in Iris's ravings.

"Say, you always wait for weekend rates. What's wrong?"

Ah, so she was cheap. A penny pincher.

"I don't know, Mom. That may not be—Hollis seemed to—I know I'm not—but Hollis—Now, Mom—"

She had yet to let him finish a sentence.

"I'm just not sure this would be the best time to come. She's pretty sick right now. No, I haven't actually *seen* her—but she wouldn't be in the hopsital if—"

What did the old bat think, Iris was faking an appendectomy? Catherine was suddenly glad she had put her shirt back on and now she rose to go. Anybody with an old crow like that for a mother had fifty percent old crow genes themselves. No wonder her mother had always advised her children to marry orphans. Turning sideways, she tried to sidle past his position in the narrow doorway and leave, but Jay fastened his arm around her waist and wouldn't let her pass. He shook his head no and gave her shirt a frustrated look as though she had just locked up the candy store by putting the garment back on.

"Well, if you're sure, I'll tell Hollis. Okay, Friday morning. We'll have a nice visit. Right. Flight 218. See you then. 'Bye."

Jay hung up the phone and placed his head against the enameled yellow woodwork of the doorframe. He explained the call, forgetting that Catherine had heard his half and was quite capable of piecing together what she had missed. "My mother's flying in Friday morning," he intoned wearily. "I just hope Hollis is wrong about the antagonism between her and Iris."

"You haven't noticed anything yourself?"

He sighed and looked at her. She was looking rather pointedly at his hand on her waist. He ignored her. His eye was giving him hell. "I can be rather oblivious to the dynamics of the interpersonal relationships around me, I'm afraid." He sounded almost apologetic. "I guess I just get too involved in my work."

A man who lost himself in his work combined with a nastily tempered mother. She must be crazy. Or masochistic. Possibly both. She'd just have to get over this *infatuation*, that's all there was to it. There was really no choice in the matter, anyway. There wasn't enough time between now and momma-in-law's arrival for Jay's interpersonal fog to clear enough for him to declare true love and undying devotion.

Jay shook his head clear of his introspections and focused his eyes on the stiffly waiting Catherine. "Rosie, I have the opposite problem around you. I can't keep my mind on anything *but* you. I smell your perfume everywhere and think of sweet, wild red roses." His head began to lower. "Now, where were we?"

But Catherine's mood had been broken. "I have to go, Jay. I'll see you tomorrow after I get home from work."

"Where do you have to rush off to?" he demanded. "It's only eight-thirty and you haven't got a date or anything. I want to experiment some more."

His choice of words was bad and stiffened her resolve. She wanted to build a relationship while he was only interested in "experiments" of the type mothers had warned their daughters about down through the ages. "Actually, I do have a date tonight and I've got to get going." It was with a package of Twinkies, but he didn't have to know that. She needed to get away and think for a while.

"Oh . . . well . . . don't let me stop you, then." His arm dropped immediately and she let herself out the back door, not seeing the forlorn and yearning gaze that followed her.

Her phone was ringing. God, was there no escaping the instrument? "Iris, is it really you? I didn't think you'd be up to phone calls yet. How are you, for God's sake? . . . If you wanted to know that, you should call Jay. He's the one that's supposed to be watching them... Yes, he's a hunk. Yeah, well, I have spent *some* time helping him out. Don't crow, it's rude. He just seemed a little unsure of himself. Hey, you're going to hurt yourself laughing like that. Hmm? Oh, sure. They're all fine. Missing their mommy, of course. We pray for you every night. God'll get you out of that hospital in self-defense.

"Jay? He's all right in a Jolly Green Giant sort of way. Iris, for heaven's sake. Take a drink of water—you sound like you're choking. I only meant he was big and kind of bumbly. No, nothing's happened, and I really don't see it happening anytime soon. Oh, I've got the inclination, make no mistake. Lord, the first time I saw him, I thought 'Wow, this is it!' But now I'm not so sure. The man's an emotional infant, you know? And I think he wants to cut his baby teeth on me. Then he's going to pack up and head for the west coast, and where would that leave me? I don't think he's thought that far ahead, but I have."

Catherine had her secret supply of Twinkies out and had removed the pitcher of iced tea from the refrigerator. She reached for a glass from the upper cabinet and carefully began to pour. "By the way, Momma-in-law plans on arriving Friday morning. Perhaps you'd better see about Hollis heading her off at the pass if she's as bad as you've said. Your rapierlike wit won't be up to snuff and you'll be no match for her until you've had a little more recovery time....

"I'm eating a Twinkie. Yes, I know it's rude to eat while talking on the phone, but I've had a rough day, so give me a break. I don't know where she's planning on sleeping, for heaven's sake. Jay talked to the woman, not me. I just overheard bits and pieces.... Get real. Nobody expects to take over the host and hostess's bed. I admit I haven't met her. Let's talk about something else, okay? Mothers-in-law. I may never marry."

After hanging up, Catherine slipped between clean sheets already warm and sticky from the muggy summer air and slept the sleep of the self-righteous. The huge bulk of a man creeping into her room in the early morning hours found her in the same position she'd gone to sleep in. Curled tightly on her side, arms crisscrossed over her chest, she hadn't budged from the fetal position.

He touched her shoulder, shaking her slightly. Catherine was instantly awake, shooting up into a sitting position, a scream dying on her lips as she recognized her assailant.

"Good God. My nerves will be shot and I'll look old and gray by the time you leave. What in blue blazes are you *doing* here?" Her left hand rested over her chest in the classic pose of someone trying to calm their heart after a fright.

"I thought someone pounding on your door at five in the morning would frighten you." Jay seemed surprised by her lack of appreciation for his thoughtfulness.

Her tongue was unguarded in her flustered condition, and she shot back sarcastically, "Yes, finding a strange man hulking over me in my bedroom is so much more reassuring than an unknown man on the other side of a locked door."

Jay looked hurt. "I don't hulk."

Catherine exhaled a deep breath and tried to get a grip on her racing emotions. "Jay, exactly why are you here? And let me warn you—make this good."

Pleased to be getting back to what he saw as the key issue, Jay sat on the edge of the bed and in a prophetic voice of doom announced, "There aren't any clean clothes."

"What?"

"The kids' drawers," he enunciated each word slowly to allow their deep significance an opportunity to sink in, "are empty. There is no clean underwear, shorts or tops with which to clothe their little bodies. It's just now connected. Nobody's done any laundry since Iris went to the hospital." He indicated his own unbuttoned, hastily donned shirt with a meaningful index finger. "I myself seem to be stuck in yesterday's shirt—and there's sand in it." He raised his eyebrows at life's cruel ploys.

Catherine sank back in the bed and pulled a pillow over her head. "Go away, Jay."

He lifted the pillow away. "This is serious, Rosie! What are we going to do?"

Why was it only "we" when there was a problem? Surely the man didn't expect her to get out of bed at five o'clock in the morning and do his laundry before putting in a full day's work? But all the while another side of her knew that was exactly what he hoped for. She and the kids weren't even related, for heaven's sake. "My suggestion to you is that you gather up the dirty clothes and run them through the machine in the basement."

"Rosie, I don't know how to use a washing machine. I've never done it before."

"The name is Catherine. Use it. And you're a Ph.D. Read the directions and figure it out," she snarled.

"Rosie," he began placatingly, as though humoring someone whose thought processes weren't quite clear. "I *told* you I wasn't much good at this kind of thing."

He'd told her all right, but was his incompetence by nature or by design? How convenient not to be able to handle life's little drudgeries.

"My housekeeper has always done it for me. You've simply got to help me out." He stripped the sheet off her body with a single-mindedness born of desperation and then froze, gaping at the display of silken limbs exposed by the nightgown's bad habit of riding up during the night.

"Hell and damnation." He spoke reverently before looking back to her face. "You better get out of that bed and start helping me with the laundry before I move onto bigger and better things." His eyes dropped significantly to the sweet swell of her curving bottom just visible beneath the hem of the gown.

"Forget it," she advised while yanking the gown down and scrambling hurriedly from the suddenly erotic confines of the bed she had peacefully slept in for years. She looked at it curiously over her shoulder while groping in a dresser drawer for clean underwear, puzzled by the sudden loss of safety she felt. She'd never rest comfortably there again. "I'm not in the mood. I have a headache."

"How can you have a headache? You just got up," he pointed out.

"You've given it to me. Now get out of here. Go gather up the laundry while I get dressed. I'll meet you in the laundry room—which is in the basement, by the way." She groaned. "I can't believe I'm doing laundry for a perfect stranger at five o'clock in the morning."

"I'm not strange," Jay returned. "Only perfect."

"That's what you think, Ph.D.," she scoffed. "Can't put a quarter in a lousy machine. And don't forget the detergent!"

Chapter Eight

Things were a bit fuzzy all day Wednesday. What with starting the day by sorting lights from darks at five in the morning, it was not surprising. Beth Anne had called in sick. Caroline, the other checker who could run the office in a pinch was on vacation until the end of the week. That meant Catherine had to man the office from 7:30 a.m. until thirty minutes after the store's posted closing time of 10:00 p.m.

To top things off, a drain in one of the refrigerator cases had backed up. The *fish* case drain, naturally. God, the whole place had stunk. She'd been tired, overburdened, and on the verge of nausea all day from the pungent fish odor produced as the crushed ice packed around the seafood had melted from the display case and backed up in the plugged drain.

The safe buzzed as she packed the last register drawer into its confines, letting her know she was behind schedule, and that the alarm company would be notifying the police if the safe wasn't hooked into their system within the next five minutes. "All right, all right. I hear you, you old hunk of junk," she muttered, talking to the metal box. She slammed the door shut and spun the combination dial. "Don't push your luck, I'm going as fast as I can." The wooden frame surrounding the strongbox was also fastened shut and keyed in. She stood in front of it impatiently tapping her foot, waiting for the confirming beep that the alarm had connected into the system and was set for the night. When it came, she sighed in relief, gathered up her purse, and punched out on her time card, marking the official end of a very long day. Anybody touching the safe from then until eight the next morning would have the police down their backs within seconds. She knew. She and Gary had popped it open five minutes too soon one morning and had spent an uncomfortable half hour with the police while they quizzed them and checked their identification. Very embarrassing.

As she made her tired way toward the store doors, Gary promised to try to make up for the hectic day.

She leaned against the cool glass of the doors, almost too tired to make the effort of pushing them open, and returned, "I'm too pooped to care. Why don't I just stay here and sleep on a checkout counter? I have to be back at seven-thirty anyway. I'll just get home in time to turn around and come back."

But Gary laughed and sent her on her way. "Look at it as a challenge. You were able to rise and meet it. You had the 'right stuff.'" He hastily changed subjects at her glare. "You haven't told me how things are going with the temblor prince. What's new? Any proposals of marriage yet?"

She thought about going home and facing the rest of the laundry and faded a little more at the prospect. "I'm thinking of changing my mind about the whole project. Proving yourself indispensable can be darn tiring." Damn. She'd forgotten to pick up disposable diapers for Tod.

Hopefully there'd be enough left to get Jay through the next day. "I'll see you tomorrow—if you're lucky," she said, more or less falling out the door into the lighted parking lot and scurrying over to her own faithful Dodge. "Take me home, flying friend," she mumbled exhaustedly as she slid across the blue vinyl seat.

Once home, she called Iris at the hospital, not caring that it was now eleven o'clock in the evening.

"Iris," she began with little preamble. "As I have neither the benefits nor the privileges that go along with being a wife and mother, I cannot understand how I have somehow gotten the responsibilities. I have had a rotten day, the prospects for tomorrow are no better, and I am not, you hear, am not going downstairs to do laundry. Call Hollis and tell him to get himself down to the laundry room and not to leave said laundry room until he has produced enough clean clothes to suitably attire his progeny for the duration."

Iris's laugh tinkled gently over the line, not at all offended by her friend's tirade. "Not to worry. I sent Hollis home once Jay mentioned the problem and told him the homefront needed him more than I did. Supposedly everything's under control again." She ignored Catherine's inelegant snort. "What I can't understand is why Jay came to you in the first place. Hollis was home until seven. I guess he assumed Hollis was as incompetent as he is. He's not, you know. I made sure he could at least load a washer and dryer before we married. *I'm* not into self-abuse."

Catherine hung up on her. Smart aleck.

But if Catherine had any worries over being too tired to function well the next day at work, they were a wasted effort. She was back home by nine that morning. After parking the car with exaggerated care, she was so benumbed that she didn't even notice Jay sitting on the next stoop down from her own entrance watching the kids whiz on trikes up and down the already hot concrete sidewalks.

Jay watched as she crossed the street to her own stoop, black-pocketed grocery smock unbuttoned and billowing around her, nameplate askew, head bent as though the asphalt beneath her feet was the most fascinating stuff she'd ever encountered. He waved and called, even half rose when she stumbled on the curb, but she didn't respond. His look was one of puzzlement as she disappeared into her foyer. Was she sick? Was business so slow she'd come home to make up for yesterday's long hours?

"Uncle Juli, will you hold me up on my two wheeler?"

"Uh, sure, pumpkin. I'll be right there." He cast a last look at the doorway that had swallowed Catherine and shrugged his shoulders, striding down the steps to steady Emi on her new eighteen-incher.

His occasional glances up to the reflective glass windows of Catherine's living room shed no light on the puzzle. Lunchtime came and Jay herded the children upstairs to eat. He was growing faintly uneasy. He'd half expected her to join him if she'd merely taken time off because business was slow. But hour after hour had slipped by with no sign from the top floor apartment. Now it was close to one o'clock. He settled the trio into bed with favorite toys and blankets and waited ten minutes outside the closed doors to make sure they had fallen asleep before slipping out the back and across the six-foot porch to Catherine's rear entrance. If he left both rear doors open, he rationalized, he'd be able to hear any movement before it got serious.

Speaking of serious—he knew Catherine strove to catch every little breeze during the few hot summer days he'd spent with her. Her rear door was sealed shut. Her apartment must be as hot as the hinges of Hades by now. He stooped to peer through the paned-glass window in the door. The distorted imperfections in the old glass gave him a wavery view of Catherine, hunched in her cane and steel-framed Breuer's chair and huddled over the small kitchen table. There were five packages of Twinkies neatly lined up in front of her. Two were empty, their cellophane wrappers tidily folded into quarters and neatly placed, each on its own small white cardboard rectangle which still displayed the two slashes of cake residue. A third was being methodically unwrapped, the cellophane wrapper carefully smoothed out on the table in preparation for folding.

Jay knocked, but Catherine didn't hear. He knocked again, more forcefully. As he prepared to bang on the door to get her attention, kick it if necessary, she looked up, as though the sound had just then registered.

Her brows knit in puzzlement as she rose to open the door. "What're you doing here, Jay? I'm on from seven until four-thirty today." Stupid thing to say. Obviously she wasn't 'on' or she'd be at the store. "How'd you even know I was home?" She seemed rather surprised to be there herself. She looked suspiciously at the dingy gray shirt he wore. "You can't be out of clean clothes already."

Jay was momentarily sidetracked by her unintended slur. "Hey, I just washed this shirt yesterday. Hollis showed me how to work the washer and dryer. I don't know what the big fuss is all about—it's not that difficult." He looked down at the shirt with pride, greatly pleased with his efforts.

Catherine made no response, too wound up in her own problems to ask if he had bothered with detergent or sorting out the whites from the darks. Right at the moment she simply didn't care that the discolored rumpled mass clinging limply to his muscled chest looked remarkably like the pristine white, crisp broadcloth shirt he had worn a few days before. So laundry wasn't his forte. Nothing seemed to be hers.

Jay zeroed in on the purpose of his visit. "For a change, I don't need anything. I came to see about you. Are you sick or something? Business slow today or what?"

Catherine's laugh was a little high-pitched and slightly hysterical. Sick or something. That was one way of putting it.

"They think I did it," she whispered in a curious voice, sinking back into her caned chair and picking up an unwrapped Twinkie. "How can they think that?"

"Who thinks you did what?" he questioned, not having the slightest inkling as to what she was talking about.

"I've worked there eight years. Ever since I was sixteen," she said accusingly, hurtingly. "And they think I would do something like that." She shook her head, crushed at the injustice of it all.

"*What* do they think you did, Rosie?" Jay squatted, trying to capture her attention by looking directly into her face and failing. Her eyes were unfocused, looking blankly down at the Twinkie in her hand and she studied it instead of him, turning it in the light as though it was a faceted jewel.

"How can they think that, Jay?" She looked up at him, her eyes wide in their hurt, asking him to explain the vagaries of life.

"Catherine Rose." His nickname for her was dropped in favor of the more formal mode of address. "Look at me." He took her shoulders and turned her toward him, then cupped her chin and aimed her face directly at his. "Stop rambling, do you hear?" He gave her a little shake as her eyes glassed over again. It brought her back. "Now exactly what happened at work this morning? What is going on?"

Catherine chewed thoughtfully on her Twinkie until Jay wanted to shake her harder in frustration. She swallowed, looked at him, and took a drink of milk to wash the crumbs down. She looked at him again and very calmly stated, "There was a surprise audit of the store this morning. The safe count was off by a thousand dollars. I was the only one in the office yesterday." She shrugged with the unconcern of one still in shock. "It couldn't have been anyone else."

Jay squatted by her side, looking thoughtful. "But I remember you saying last time that you never worried over large missing amounts. That nobody could lose that much and it was always in the paperwork. You only worried about tens or twenties because you actually could have done something wrong with a little amount like that. Don't worry, it'll show up."

"That's what I thought," Catherine responded in that curious, flat monotone. "But I've gone over everything with a fine-tooth comb, and I can't find any errors. The registers were within pennies of being even, the office drawer was even, the deposits match the sales receipts exactly. If I took money from the safe and forgot to minus it off the safe inventory, it would have shown up as an overage somewhere. Don't you see? It's simply disappeared."

"That's ridiculous."

"Tell that to them."

"Them who? Who are them?"

"The powers that be. The head heads. Mr. Vincent himself eventually showed up, shaking his head sorrowfully and looking dolefully at me as though he had expected better and I had let him down."

Jay was thinking out loud as he continued squatting at her side. "Maybe the money was gone before you went in yesterday."

Catherine shook her head regretfully. "The person opening the office for the day is responsible for doing a physical inventory of the safe money. The money in the safe matched the inventory sheet yesterday morning. I know. I counted it myself."

"Maybe you miscounted. You seemed rather bleary-eyed when you left here yesterday morning."

She gave him a speaking glance—one that asked whose fault that was—before haughtily saying, "I could count money accurately in my sleep. I've at least figured out what's missing and there's no way I would have not missed a thousand dollars in twenties."

Jay rose, at a loss for an explanation. He stamped his foot to ease the pins and needles and sank gratefully into the chair opposite Catherine's. Giving his foot a final shake, he leaned forward, resting his elbows on the butcher-block table, and requested, "Start at the beginning. Tell me everything that's happened since you left here this morning. Every detail, in sequence." He grabbed a Twinkie before she could and took a bite. "Shoot."

Catherine gathered her thoughts as she unwrapped a fresh package. She picked one up, prepared to take a bit and then seemed to realize what she was doing. Carefully she set it back down and looked at the empty wrappers surrounding her in surprise. How had she eaten so many? She'd probably die of sucrose overdose before the afternoon was over. "Let's see," she began. "I got up at six and washed my hair—"

"I think we can skip this part," Jay interrupted dryly. "Start with when you locked your car in the store parking lot."

"Oh. I thought you wanted each and every intimate gory detail."

"The parking lot?" he prompted.

"Right. The parking lot. Well, let's see. I locked the door and put the keys into my smock pocket. Then I yelled at Gary that it wasn't seven-thirty yet. His watch picks up time, you see, and he's always trying to pop the door alarm too soon. Then again, he could be doing it just to get me going. Who knows with him? I certainly don't. There was one time—"

Jay groaned and rolled his eyes and mumbled under his breath, "God in heaven, I don't believe this. What I'd give for a succinct, scientific, *factual* report right now. Okay, so now you're in the store, entering the booth. Now what?" He bit his Twinkie viciously in two, fortifying himself for the rest of the saga.

"You don't want to hear about the coffee machine taking my money and giving me coffee without a cup?"

"Damn it, Rosie—"

Catherine laughed a little halfheartedly, finally coming out of her fog a little. "Just kidding, Jay. Just kidding."

"Thank God," he snorted. "I was beginning to worry about you. That's the last time I ask for details. Just give me the essentials instead, and I'll ask for details as I need them."

Catherine gave a humorless laugh. "Okay, here it is, short and sweet. Seven thirty-five. I've punched in, had my coffee, and I'm in the office. I work on the previous day's sales for about twenty minutes and everything is working out to the penny, which is to say, each register's department-by-department readings—you know, bakery, deli, meat and grocery—of the night before is adding up to exactly what the checker took in on her register minus her initial setup cash of fifty dollars and plus or minus whatever she was over or short. Nobody was off by more than a few pennies yesterday. Since each register's checks, coupons and excess cash is turned into the office throughout the day and then the whole drawer is dumped into mine at the end of the day as they leave, my drawer, plus the extra money I deposited into the secured part of the safe for Armor pickup should equal the sales for the entire store minus the new banks I make up for each register to start the next day with and plus the money I gave out for bottle returns. In other words, the totals of the readings taken from all the registers all added together are accounted for. Are you with me so far?''

"Barely.'' Jay's head was starting to spin with the details of grocery store office work. "Did I actually once tell you this was a no-mind type of job? I apologize for any disparaging remarks I may have made in the past.''

Catherine nodded her head regally. "Apology accepted. But the truth is, you just have to be detail-minded, not a super-brain.''

Jay had his doubts about that, but now was not the time. "Go on,'' he directed.

"As I said, it was all working out beautifully, no discrepancies of any sort when Gary lets himself into the office like he does every morning to open the safe for the day. It's the same ritual every day. I didn't even turn around when I heard him come in. I tell him it's too early. He asks how I know. I say I'm not done with the paperwork. It takes me exactly thirty minutes to do the paperwork, provided there aren't any problems—therefore, since I haven't hit any snags, it can't be eight o'clock yet and why doesn't he get a watch that works?''

"And why doesn't he?'' Jay was admittedly curious.

"Says he doesn't need one with me around.'' She shrugged.

"Huh, he's got a point. Go on.''

"Well, he says all of that, and *then* he totally surprised me by saying something like, 'Isn't she amazing the way she can tell time by where she is in the paperwork, Fred?' And I

turned around to find another man in the office with him!''
She shook her head, still upset by the day's deviation from
the normal routine and began to fold and refold the Twinkie wrappers on the table in front of her.

"And this was...?" Jay prompted, placing his hand over
hers to still it.

"And this was a surprise auditor brought in by the chain's
hierarchy. Brought in to go through each store's books and
check up on the employees, I guess.''

Jay sat back, looking satisfied. "Ah, now we're getting
somewhere. Then what happened?'' He let go of her hand.
Physically touching her was too distracting when he was
trying to concentrate. "And leave that cellophane alone.''

"The safe beeped at exactly eight o'clock, which is the
alarm company's way of letting us know they're discon-
necting for the day and I told Gary to go ahead and open
it.''

"While the auditor was going over your work?''

"No, I wasn't quite finished yet. So Gary offered to count
the money in the safe and check it against the inventory for
me. I said fine, the auditor said, no, he'd do it. I said fine.''

Jay hazarded a guess. "But everything wasn't fine.''

"Not exactly,'' Catherine grimaced. "Two bundles of
twenties were missing. Kaput. Vanished.''

"I get the idea.''

"The auditor said, 'You're missing a thousand dollars
here.' I told him that was impossible—I'd just finished the
sales report, see, and everything had worked out to the
penny. If the safe was actually a thousand short, the sales
should have been a thousand over, follow? If it was a paper
error, that is.''

"Uh-huh. Go ahead. I'm muddling along here as best I
can.'' He crossed his legs in front of him and frowned as he
concentrated on the story.

"That's it." She gave a deprecatory shrug. "We re-counted three times, went through the figures twice. It's simply not there."

"And you were the only one in the office yesterday, so by process of elimination, you've been crowned thief of the day and cast out while they investigate, is that it?"

"Close enough," she agreed, slumping back into her chair and gazing helplessly at the four walls around her.

"And you can't put the cash back because you don't have it?"

"Jay..." His name was long, drawn out, and accusative.

"I wasn't asking, exactly. More stating a fact."

"It didn't sound that way," she stated suspiciously. "Do you think I stole the money?"

"Now, Rosie. As you have pointed out, we don't know each other all that well."

"Do you think I stole the money, Jay? A simple yes or no will suffice." She rose from her chair, looking at him long and hard.

He returned her gaze for a full minute. "No," he said, his voice sure. "I know you didn't take it."

She sank back in her chair, relieved with that, at least. "What if it doesn't show up?" she questioned mournfully.

"It will," he assured her maddeningly and stretched his arms and shoulders upward in a most distracting manner. "If you were indeed the only one in the office and you didn't take it, it's got to be there somewhere. In the meantime, you've got several unexpected days off. And while I wouldn't want to sound callous or uncaring, I could really use your help."

Well, it certainly sounded callous and uncaring to her. She rose and put her cup in the sink and her Twinkie papers in the garbage. Men, she disparaged, could only think in terms of how a situation affected them. She nibbled a fingernail thoughtfully as she considered whether to let him get away with it and flinched as the nail ripped below the cuticle.

"Look what you've done. You shouldn't bite your nails like that," Jay directed. "It's a bad nervous habit."

Her shoulders hunched defensively and she wondered about pointing out the obvious as she took in his blinking eye. Deciding against it, she turned to leave the room. "You'd better go check on the kids," she said instead. "I'm going in to stare at the bedroom ceiling and rack my brains." She tapped her head thoughtfully. "Whatever happened yesterday is up here somewhere. All I have to do is draw it out. Some little mistake..." She let the sentence die out.

Jay turned her back and said, "Thank you."

"What for?" she questioned, surprised.

"For not throwing my eye back at me when I inexcusably mentioned your nail biting."

She nodded and his eyes were caught by her gracefully undulating hair. "It's okay."

"It isn't, either. You know—"

His thought was interrupted as the back door swung open and Hollis entered the room. He was as large as his brother, and Catherine felt dwarfed as the two men crowded into the small kitchen. "Thought I'd find you here," he said to his brother. "I've managed to finish up the safety testing on the model car paint I had to get done at the lab and I've taken the rest of the day off. Instead of spending it at Iris's bedside, who is getting decidedly testy and unfun, I thought I'd give you two a break and take my own kids for the afternoon." The offer was made magnanimously. "So why don't you take the rest of the day and go do something by yourselves for awhile?" He puffed up his chest and looked from one to the other as if expecting laudits for his magnanimity.

But even he couldn't miss noticing the heavy atmosphere in the room. "What's wrong?" he finally queried.

"Nothing," Jay hastened to assure him as tears glistened in Catherine's eyes as she thought about the morning's disasters. "Catherine's had a bit of a problem at work, that's all."

That was all? If it was *his* job, it would've been more than a "bit of a problem," she bet.

"Since you're home, I'll spend my time keeping her mind off her troubles. I'm sure it'll clear up by itself. Just one of those things, you know."

Hollis didn't know, of course, but he obligingly began backing out of the room while his now puzzled glance swung between the two of them. "Well, okay," he offered uncertainly. "I'll just go check on the little seraphim—" He stopped cold and looked at his brother. "I've just thought of something." He spoke as if the hammer of doom hung over his head.

"What? Good Lord, what's wrong now?"

"Mother's coming tomorrow morning."

"I know that. I'm the one who gave you the message," Jay chided.

"Okay, you think you're so smart. Where are we going to put her?"

Jay had to admit he had him there. He tended to forget about the practicalities until he got hit over the head with them. He thought about the problem for a moment. His mother was not the type to take being put on the sofa in the living room while he used the guest room. And Jay was a good twelve or more inches longer than the sofa. "I'll move in with Rosie, here," Jay began tentatively. "She's got a spare bedroom. She won't mind." He turned to see the growing cloud banks forming over Catherine's brow. "Uh, will you, Rosie?"

Catherine viewed him in astonishment. "Surely you jest."

Jay seemed a little less certain. "Well, no. Not really. What's wrong with the idea?"

"What's wrong with the idea!" *The wicked witch of the west was on her way and he was going to move into her apartment just in time for her arrival?* "I'll tell you what's wrong. What do you think your mother is going to think of me when she finds her son living in my apartment?"

Jay was somewhat taken aback at her obvious strong feelings on the matter. Her eyes snapped and her rich brown hair swirled in a tempest, foaming around her head. His mother could be a tad judgmental, but she wasn't *that* bad. At least not that he'd ever noticed. "Now, Rosie, calm down. Why would my mother be upset at my staying with you? I'm not going to lay a finger on you. What would she have to object to?"

Catherine shook her head and closed her eyes in her disbelief at his naïveté. She began in the tone originally designed for explaining the facts of life to a particularly dim-witted child. It didn't last long. "Jay." Her voice was already on the ascendant. "What mother in her right mind is going to believe that? *I* don't even believe it." She was yelling by then.

He was clearly insulted. Drawing up to his full height, he stared down at her. "I said I wouldn't touch you, and I won't. I don't give my word loosely." His entire stance dared her to call him a liar.

But now Catherine was too insulted herself to bother. Her rage took a new tack. "And just exactly why wouldn't you touch me if we were living together, I'd like to know? Just you answer me that! What's wrong with me? Hmm? There are plenty of men out there who would be perfectly willing to be cooped up in an apartment with me, let me tell you. And there wouldn't be a damn platonic thing about it.

You're back into your intellectual snob routine again, aren't you? I'm not good enough for you. I don't have a Ph.D. Of course your mother would assume our relationship was perfectly innocent. Who'd ever believe the great Dr. Gand might be messing around with an unemployed grocery clerk? Well, you'll move in here over my dead body, buddy." She gave him her back, crossing her arms defensively in front of her and tapping an angry tattoo with her foot. It was ineffective in her rubber-soled shoes, but Jay got the idea.

He sank back down into the kitchen chair, amazed that she could be somehow insulted by what he saw as an offer of gentlemanly behavior.

Hollis noted philosophically, "Hell hath no fury like a woman scorned, and all of that. You've been getting away with murder for years, old man. It's time you knew what the rest of us deal with on a daily basis."

Jay sank back into the chair, staring at the tabletop in front of him as though the conundrum of convoluted logic Catherine had just served up was sitting there in front of him, waiting for him to rearrange the pieces and make some sense of the puzzle. "Rosie," he started cautiously, unsure of exactly how to proceed. "I never meant to infer you were somehow unworthy of my...my...uh, attentions." He stopped to glare at Hollis as he made a choking sound over by the back door. Hollis was evidently enjoying his brother's predicament and seemed intent on seeing how he worked his way out from under the wrath of a wounded female's ire. Jay frowned and jerked his head toward the door, indicating he wanted Hollis to leave, but Hollis pretended not to understand and stood his ground. Jay frowned more fiercely.

Rising from the chair, Jay crossed the narrow room to set an arm across Catherine's trembling shoulder and was amazed to hear her actually sniffling. He at least had the tact not to notice as she brushed angrily at her eyes with a balled fist. Pulling her more tightly to his side, he tried again. "Ah, Catherine Rose, how you can question your desirability is beyond me. Didn't our few sessions on the sofa tell you anything? There's nothing I'd like better than to finish what we started. I just thought you'd want me to be a gentleman while staying in your home. You'd be doing Iris a great favor and I wouldn't want to take advantage of you in return."

It was obvious by the way Hollis snapped to attention that he was taking in the content of Jay's soliloguy with great interest. What sibling wouldn't be interested to find his sainted brother had been doing more than entertaining three little children?

Jay turned her frontwise and pushed her head firmly into his shirt where he could feel the tears he had only suspected wetting his skin through the thin fabric. Kissing the top of her head, he murmured softly, "Now I don't want you worrying about any of this. Hollis and I will work it out. I don't want Mom thinking badly of you. Not that she would, but we won't take the chance, all right? The sofa will be just fine for me."

Catherine sniffed and nodded her head in compliance. Hollis left, looking like he was going to burst out laughing at the slightly desperate look Jay gave him. Jay hadn't quite pulled it off. He'd gotten back in Catherine's good graces, but it would be clear to a brother that he had been hoping she would relent with something to the effect of "Oh, no, Jay. That sofa is much too short. Of course you can stay here."

Better luck next time.

Chapter Nine

When Hollis finally slipped out the back door, Jay drew Catherine with him into the living room, opening up every window he passed. He settled into the navy waleless corduroy sofa with her still safely in tow. Jay combed her hair away from her face with his fingers and left them on the sides of her head, tenderly holding her. He spoke soothingly. "Ah, Rosie, love, don't be upset. You counted the money yesterday morning when the safe was opened, right?"

She nodded mutely. It was a small nod, as Jay still firmly held her head.

"And no one else was in the office all day?"

Again she nodded.

He brought his lips down to lightly brush her moist mouth and he whispered caressingly, cajolingly, "Well, then, there's nothing to worry about, is there? You didn't take it, so it has to show up somewhere along the line. Now I happen to know the perfect way to take your mind off your troubles.'' His lips darted, pausing only long enough to place butterfly light kisses all over her finely drawn, pale cheeks. ''Want me to continue the demonstration?''

Catherine still looked dazed, but she settled herself more comfortably in his lap, looped her arms around his neck and tried to enter into the spirit of things. ''You mean you had already started trying to take my mind off my troubles? That was it?''

He reached behind his neck to loosen her hold and drew the work smock she still wore down her arms, dropping it over the edge of the sofa. ''Your nameplate was jabbing me,'' he told her, his smile slow and rather wolflike. ''I couldn't really concentrate on the job at hand.''

She was pleased he knew she'd only been teasing. It was a good omen. ''Perhaps you need the sterile atmosphere of a science lab to properly concentrate.''

It was obvious he was learning not to take her every word so seriously. His smile never wavered and his fingers teased the edge of the hot pink blouse she had worn underneath her smock. When he began edging *that* up and out of his way, she wondered what could have been jabbing him there. His index finger drew a tantalizing line of fire on the exposed skin at the top of her navy gabardine cullotte waistband. ''It's very warm in here,'' he whispered enticingly as he shimmied the hem of her blouse up a further tad and waved it a bit to produce a small breeze that played across her stomach.

Catherine was caught in the hypnotic power of his blue gaze, and she responded absently, ''Yes. It is rather warm, isn't it?'' She didn't seem to realize that the fine film beginning to break out on her upper lip had nothing to do with the air temperature.

Jay let it go. His attention was taken with the tantalizing glimpses of smooth flesh being exposed as the blouse wafted up and down. "Oh, my God," he muttered as the underswell of her breast came momentarily into view. "You haven't got a bra on." Gathering his courage, he eased her blouse up completely and rested his hands on her shoulders, holding her slightly away from him as he speechlessly studied her naked torso.

"So beautiful," he finally whispered, staring at the twin swollen peaks capped in rosy pebbled hardness. But as his lightly callused fingers reached for their beckoning sweetness, Catherine held out her hand.

"No, wait," she remonstrated.

She twisted in his lap and leaned to work the two buttons on the placket of his knit shirt. His face began to flush as her breasts rubbed gently against him as she manipulated the buttons to complete her task. Catherine worried her bottom lip with straight white teeth as she concentrated and Jay moaned, finally knocking her hands away to strip first her blouse and then his own shirt over their respective heads in hasty, jerky motions that spoke of his inner turmoil.

Catherine leaned into him more fully, pushing him backward. He toppled willingly back into the sofa cushions. But he took her with him, refusing to release his grip. She tumbled on top of him, breathing in the clean lemon hint of his soap, basking in the liquid warmth of his gaze. Regaining her balance, she raised herself up, propped herself on her arms and lightly rubbed her nipples through the abrasive crisp hair that grew in thick abundance across the breadth of his chest.

He clasped her sides and pulled her more aggressively through the crisp thicket, ending her slow tantalizing motions. His eyes were closed and his words came on a harsh rasp. "God, Rosie, you feel so good. All silk and satin. Hot passion beneath an oh-so-proper exterior. A man could drown in you and not bother putting up much of a struggle on the way down.''

She had never thought of herself as particularly passionate. His words amazed her. But it must be true, for as he pulled her higher on his body and began to worry her warm breast with kisses, it was all she could do to keep from crying out her pleasure.

Judging by the labored breathing and the changing contours beneath her, Jay was not exactly immune to the passions raging between them, either. Catherine loved knowing she was responsible for every little catch in his breath even as she was amazed by her temerity, letting her hands wander where they willed. She noted with pleasure the change in his breathing as she finally homed in on the top snap of his jeans. She pulled it free, but left the zipper alone. Instead, she let a finger roam under the fabric, letting it weave through the warm crisp hair still hidden from view. Jay sucked in his already flat stomach and didn't move, afraid of scaring away the roving probe now just inches from the center of his heat.

But the jeans didn't allow enough leeway and Catherine retreated, putting her head down on his chest and luxuriating in the feel of hard muscle covered in cushioning fur beneath her cheek. She could hear his heart pounding under her ear, clearly pumping under stress. The temperature in the room seemed to be still rising and a fine sheen of perspiration covered them both.

''Oh, my wild Rose, I want you so badly right now,'' Jay whispered as his tongue investigated her ear. ''I want this to be perfect for both of us. Tell me what you want, how you like it . . . everything.''

Catherine froze in his arms, but Jay seemed not to notice as his hands roamed her backside, lightly skimming the surface in an action guaranteed to have raised goose bumps only moments before. "Tell me, Rosie," he urged.

In her consternation, she propped herself up so that she could look down into his face, searching it. "Don't you know, Jay?"

Her raised position brought her breasts into perfect position. Just the slightest maneuver allowed Jay to bury his face in the scented valley between the two perfectly shaped globes. His curiously muffled voice responded, "How could I know? I've never made love to you before."

Her arms were trembling, both from what Jay was doing and the strain of supporting her upper body while he did it. "I thought men knew these things." She was beginning to have serious second thoughts here.

Jay finally detected the worry in her voice, and he lay back to look up at the shifting, unsure composition of her features. The muscle at the corner of his eye kicked in. "I've never really been all that concerned with pleasing anyone before, Rosie. It was all just a game back in college. I had to work my buns off in graduate school, and that's where I developed this damn tick. When I think back, I guess it was more an assumption on my part that girls would be turned off more than anything anyone actually said or did, but the end result was the same... What I'm trying to say is, it's been a while and even then—Well, I just don't think hot-blooded collegians are noted for their finesse in these matters. So talk to me, even though I realize nice girls don't talk about such things. It will make things a whole lot more enjoyable for both of us."

Catherine looked down in astonishment. He hadn't made love since he was in college? Lord, talk about the blind leading the blind. She sat all the way up. "Uh, Jay..."

"Yes?" he prompted. He watched her hands flutter in mute little helpless gestures. She was so damn cute in her earnestness, even if he did get the definite impression she was about to call a halt to the proceedings.

"It's just that, well, to tell you the truth . . . I don't know how I like it." Her anxious blue eyes met the warmth of his own gaze before dropping back to her fidgeting fingers. "I mean, I've never actually done this before and I kind of thought *you* would know what to do." Now she studied the ceiling. "I guess I've always been under the impression it was a fairly straightforward operation. Tab A more or less designed in heaven for slot B, if you get my drift . . ."

Jay leaned back into the sofa's cushions, his mouth literally hanging open. He'd thought her cute. Cute? Hell, she was adorable! His confidence grew. Compared to her, he was a walking, talking encyclopedia on the subject of making love, a veritable fund of information. Tab A into slot B, indeed. Good God. He was trying hard not to chuckle out loud with his pleasure in her innocence. It made him sound like he was developing a stutter. "Actually . . . there's a little more to it than . . . that, Rosie."

"I knew that."

"I'm sure. Just humor me, all right?" When she remained silent, he continued. "There has to be a certain amount of loveplay first. It feels good, draws out the action, and makes everything, um, do-able."

"What's that supposed to mean?"

"Well, tab A can get fairly large at . . . those special times. If a woman isn't properly relaxed, it can be, well, uncomfortable.

Catherine backed away several inches. She picked up her blouse and held it in front of her breasts. Her gaze dropped down to the bulge beneath his jeans and her eyes widened in alarm. Goodness. Just exactly *how* large were we talking here?

She retreated noticeably further down the sofa. "Uh, listen, Jay. I'm not sure this is really such a hot idea." Her eyes were dilated in concern. "I mean, frankly, I have some doubts as to whether the two of us—if it's even physically *possible*. Maybe someone closer to my own size... Oh, I don't know."

Her eyes were stuck on his lap, her brain still not believing its visual input. She slipped her blouse over her head. No, this would never do. She'd never actually *heard* of anyone getting permanently stuck in an indelicate position, but one never knew. This was all the proof she needed that God was male. Only a man could come up with such a system.

Jay was sorry that she was so obviously calling a halt to things, but he understood completely. And, to be truthful, the cause for her concern was a bit of an ego lift. She did that a lot for him. And seeing her hesitation, he was a little relieved to have a bit of a reprieve. The ever-present scientist in him felt a little further research at the local library might be in order before he would feel confident to allay her fears. He began to laugh at the circumstances in which he was caught.

"I'm not finding this particularly amusing, Jay," Catherine informed him. Her blouse was not only on, but tucked in, as well. She stood next to the sofa and glared down at him.

He picked up her hand and kissed her palm. "Oh, honey, I'm not laughing at you. The joke's on me, when you stop to think about it. All these years, I've been afraid of rejection because of my eye. I thought a woman would be automatically turned off. Now here I am with a beautiful woman who claims not to be fazed by that, instead she's all uptight over the size of my... my... well, the size of which a man is generally proud. The whole thing is too unbelievable to put properly into words."

Catherine blushed, and Jay thought she looked wonderful in pink. She looked great any way he'd seen her so far. "As far as I know, the system's been working just fine for a millennium or more and there's no reason to suspect it won't keep right on working. But no need to rush. We'll get some good books and see what they say about a situation like this. Who knows? They may even come with step-by-step diagrams."

He was teasing her, but she was too nervous to properly appreciate his attempt at humor. This was all just a bit too much for her. The man wanted to read *diagrammatical* dirty books with her? Good grief. But the more she thought about it . . . it just might be a whole lot more fun than gravestone rubbings.

His confidence was high enough at that point that he pulled her back down into his lap before she even made her reply. "Relax, Rosie. We'll work things out." He hugged her hard, and her breath whooshed out. "No need to search out a man your size—they don't come that little. We'll be just fine, you'll see."

"Maybe we ought to take a wait-and-see attitude," she said a little desperately as he began kissing the column of her neck. "There's always the chance one might turn up."

"If one does, he can just forget it," he murmured in return. "I saw you first."

Jay leaned to touch his toes in the clear morning air. He squatted, extending a long, lightly furred leg behind him in the traditional jogger's stretch. Catherine looked him over in the timeless manner a woman or man has used through the ages when examining a particularly vital looking specimen of the opposite sex. And this one looked good. Very good. Was it possible that he was posing for her? He'd come banging on her door bright and early that morning, claiming she needed the benefits of an anxiety-reducing, tension-lowering early morning run. She'd doubted it at the time, and was further inclined toward disbelief once she realized that evidently, the seemingly ever-radiant Susan also suffered from stress. Unfortunately, stressed out or not, she looked damn cute, just as she had since Catherine first laid eyes on her the evening before.

Susan had called from her hotel around suppertime last night and shown up with "some important papers that just couldn't wait" shortly thereafter. Catherine thoroughly suspected that Susan was more than a tad interested in Jay herself. The woman positively beamed whenever Jay directed a remark in her direction. Tsunami, p waves, ordering late-night Chinese—it didn't seem to matter. She beamed. And she was darling when she beamed, no doubt about it. The only saving grace as far as Catherine was concerned was that while the woman was obviously extremely intelligent—she knew her temblors—it was also obvious she'd shaken a screw or two loose while living on top of the San Andreas fault.

Getting Susan back to her hotel the night before had turned into a major challenge. She'd locked her rental car keys inside the car. It had taken Catherine quite a while to prod the door open with a coat hanger—no way was she going to allow the other woman to stay the night on such a flimsy excuse.

The "important papers" had been left back at the hotel, only Catherine spotted them on the back seat of the car just as Susan and Jay were pulling away from the curb to go get them. The poor thing had been so grateful to Catherine for sparing her a drive on unfamiliar streets, Catherine felt sure it hadn't been a ploy to be alone with Jay.

But best of all, Susan didn't seem to have any idea how to attract Jay's attention except with that consistent showing of her admittedly magnificent pearly whites. And she did wear clothes well. Catherine took in the other girl's coordinated aqua and peach running shorts and top. Her long blond mane was pulled back into a thick ponytail that swung jauntily through the rear opening of a pristine white terry visor. Her feet were shod in impossibly clean aqua and white running shoes. Catherine conceded defeat on this front. Even Susan's socks coordinated perfectly.

Ruefully, Catherine looked down at her own faded sport shorts. Long ago they had been white with perky red racing stripes down the side. Now both tones were washed out, faded into a murky middle ground. Her overly large T-shirt featured a computer printout of Santa in his sled, flying high with the assistance of his eight able-bodied deer. Jay had bought it for her at Santa's Village. It was supposed to have made the day worth her while. At the time, it had. Now, well... She sighed quietly to herself and went through the limbering exercises the other two seemed to have down pat. Wouldn't you know they'd been together long enough to have a pre-run sequence perfectly researched and developed? There was probably a scientific reason behind Susan even rubbing the bridge of her nose like she was just then. Stimulated her sinuses, or something equally revolting, Catherine supposed. The thing was, she still looked cute even while doing *that*!

After about a mile Catherine realized she had made a grave error in not asking just how long a run it took before one was properly invigorated and had reduced one's stress loads to a manageable level. She was starting to run out of steam, and the dynamic duo trotting politely at her side were obviously just sticking with her out of politeness. They weren't even breathing hard and Susan kept looking over her shoulder and glancing nervously around as though she didn't want anyone seeing this pathetic display. Too polite

to say anything, Catherine assumed. Susan's stress levels
were going to have trouble reducing themselves at this rate.

Jay began working on her, "Let's pick up the pace a bit,
shall we, ladies? It'll take almost an hour to cover five miles
at this rate."

Five miles? Good God. No way. "Listen, you two,"
Catherine huffed. "I'll finish up another mile or so." *Or so,
baloney. A couple more minutes, and that would be it.* "At
a slightly slower pace." *Like a crawl.* It was killing her to
send Jay off with Susan, but it was either that and live to
fight another day, or die right here and now, leaving him to
her by default. "You two go ahead at your own rate and I'll
catch you later on today." The other woman already had
several years' head start on her. How much difference could
a few more hours make?

Jay felt obliged to protest. "No, no, we can't do that. If
you would just push yourself a little bit every day, pretty
soon you'll be doing a nine-minute mile, then an eight—"

"Jay, sweetie, I run to use up calories so I can take in
more Twinkies. Period. I don't care if I *ever* do an eight-
minute mile. You're just going to have to accept that I'm
quite content wallowing in my mediocrity."

Actually he didn't have to accept it. He could just leave,
but she chose not to think about that just yet. She had another day or two left.

"She's got a point," Susan said, although no one had
been talking to her. The resident pain in Catherine's neck
sounded only slightly winded. "We shouldn't impose our
own standards of excellence on others."

After a remark like that, Catherine put the pain Susan
gave her considerably lower in her anatomy. What made it
truly painful was, the woman was trying to be *nice* and let
her off the hook! Unfortunately Susan's remarks only rein-
forced every childhood insecurity Catherine had ever been

plagued by. She was dumb. She couldn't perform. It seemed
she couldn't even run. Her heart sank into her mud-
spattered sneakers. Her lungs hurt and she wondered how
she could have gotten out of shape so fast. It had only been
a week since she'd last gone out by herself. But then, a certain amount of her current breathlessness might be attrib-
utable to her heart and lungs being squeezed by the
possibility that Jay had not been as free to do all the wonderful things they'd done together as he'd acted...Her whole
chest constricted at the thought. She gave up nose breathing and sucked air in through her mouth in an effort to bring
in more oxygen. She studied Jay out of the corner of her
eye, trying to read his sincerity. She ended up laughing at the
pained look she found on his face as he plodded patiently at
her side.

"Jay," she chuckled. "Go ahead. I swear I don't mind."
What a lie. A fault line would open up right there at her feet
and swallow her whole.

"You're sure?" It sounded more hopeful than inquiring.

She was feeling generous. "I'm sure." He looked as if he
was going to continue arguing. She cut him off. "Sweetheart, darling, light of my life," she began. "Note how I'm
starting to wheeze as I talk. I have hit the wall, as the saying goes and I would consider it a great personal favor if you
would consent to go on without me."

Catherine had already showered and changed into crisp
white shorts and a lightweight red blouse on which she had
left the top *three* buttons undone—and just happened to be
out with a book on her front stoop catching the late-
morning rays when Jay and Susan returned. The glistening
sheen on their bodies testified to the hard workout they had
been through. Jay—and Susan, she admitted grudgingly—
looked fantastic. His skin looked oiled and his muscles rip-

pled just beneath the gleaming surface. Her mouth went dry as they stopped right in front of the concrete step where she sat. What a beautiful, beautiful man.

They chatted with Catherine for a few moments, just long enough for Susan to drop a few guileless remarks that managed to point out all Catherine's inadequacies as an athlete, a woman, and a person in general. Knowing it was being done innocently and without malice did *not* help. It still hurt.

Mercifully, Jay soon walked Susan to the curb where her sporty little red rental car waited. Catherine overheard him mentioning plans for dinner for seven o'clock that evening. She should have taken her chances on her lungs bursting and stuck with them.

Jay came away from the car after fishing Susan's keys out of the street when she accidentally dropped them. The little red two-seater pulled away and Jay sat on the steps a small distance from Catherine. She supposed he was aware of his need for a shower, at least she hoped that was why he hadn't sat too close. Acting as though he hadn't just asked another woman out right in front of her, he said, "I didn't sleep at all last night, Rosie."

Don't get your hopes up, she advised herself. Without a doubt, it's not what you're thinking. "No?" she questioned.

"No. The sofa is a foot and a half too short for me and so soft you sink right into the cushions and practically suffocate."

See? "Is that right?"

"That's right." He nodded his head emphatically. "And it's all your fault."

Catherine shot him a disbelieving look. "I didn't pick out the sofa. I don't see how it can be my fault."

"But you do have a guest room," he pointed out logi-
cally. "One that is currently empty. One which I have asked
if I couldn't please use." He pursued his thoughts further.
"Why don't I stop off someplace, pick up some wine and
Twinkies and come over after everything's settled down at
Hollis's, say ten-thirty or eleven?"

"I don't think so." The man was unbelievably bold. She'd
saved his . . . neck repeatedly over the past few days with the
kids and she got Twinkies and in all probability, red ripple,
while Susan got dinner on the town? Over her dead body.

Jay gave her a exasperated look before using the front of
his shirt to wipe his dripping face. "Why the hell not? You
enjoyed our time alone together as much as I did." He
looked suddenly vulnerable. "Didn't you?"

"I loved it," she returned simply. "But I'm beginning to
see my mother might have been right when she told me over
and over that men were different from girls and that their
emotions didn't have to be involved for them to be able
to . . . perform, because, frankly, if you cared for me at all,
you wouldn't be asking me to do something that would
damage your mother's opinion of me."

Jay was clearly surprised by her soft comeback and
seemed at a loss as to how to combat her homely logic.

"But I'll tell you what I *will* do," she continued, trying to
look calm while her stomach churned. "I'll extend an invitation to your mother to stay with me tonight. That will
separate her from Iris and give everyone a bed and a break.
How's that?"

"That will never work," Jay protested, blustering.

"Why not?"

"Because—I don't—that is—"

"Oh, come on. You can introduce us right after you're
done cleaning up and I'll ask her." She turned her attention back to her book, thereby dismissing him.

Jay must have been *really* sweaty since it was a good two and a half to three hours before he came to get her. She'd been making up her guest bed when she'd heard the back door open and quietly close. The heavy footsteps out in the small kitchen almost gave her heart failure, which was immediately followed by irritation. If she had permanent cardiac damage by the time he went back to California from the sudden appearances he insisted on making in her apartment, she'd search the entire state until she found him. Then she'd sue. "For heaven's sake, can't you use the doorbell when you know I'm home, instead of scaring me half out of my wits?" The words were flung at him as she swung out of the bedroom.

"Oh. Uh, I'm sorry."

He was so obviously reluctant to be there, her heart sank. Had Susan somehow come enough out of her fog to get through to him? "Uh, so am I." She had her hand over her heart trying to calm its palpitations. "You've got to stop doing that."

"I'll be gone in just a few days," he told her encouragingly. "And then you won't have to worry about me barging in on you anymore."

That was supposed to make her feel better?

"Mom's been giving Iris...advice...on possible improvements in her, uh, child-rearing techniques and also some...tips, you know, *suggestions* on redecorating her apartment. She seems to have momentarily run out of ideas, so I guess now is as good a time as any to introduce you."

Meaning that maybe, if they hurried, they'd get to her while she was still out of breath.

"You know, I never realized how very *directive* my mother could be. Hollis says she's always been this way, that I just always had my nose buried in a book." He wiped sweaty palms on his navy cotton shorts. "Well, let's get this thing over and done with."

It sounded as though he'd prefer being caught with one leg on either side of an active fault line, all with no seismograph in sight. But no point in worrying. As he'd so graciously pointed out, he and his mother would be permanently out of stock on any shelf she'd be stocking after the next few days. She squared her shoulders. "Okay. I'm ready."

Jay looked at her askance. "Aren't you going to brush your hair? Maybe a little lipstick or something? What about your shoes?"

Catherine's toes curled as she felt the beginnings of every childhood insecurity she'd ever even considered having start working on her psyche again. She struggled to push them out of her way. "Hey, let's lighten up here. She doesn't have to stay with me if I totally offend her royal personage. I'm offering her a bed for a couple of nights, not a lifetime commitment."

"But Mom knows we've been spending a lot of time together, what with the way you've been helping me with the kids."

Big of him to give her a little credit there.

"And Hollis has added to the problem by intimating in front of Mother that there may be more than neighborliness to our, uh, relationship."

Hollis had probably just been trying to get himself and Iris off the hook by providing diversionary tidbits, the rotter. "Is that right?"

"Well, yes. Of course, I told her who your parents were and that helped. But I'd really like for you to make a good impression."

"Why?"

There was a distinctly helpless air about Jay as he pivoted and began to pace agitatedly. His eyes searched all around the room as though he might find the meaning of life written on a dustball in one of the kitchen's corners. Darn his hide. She would not buy approval on her parent's recognizance. She would not have Jay doing it for her, either. Who was he that he had her even considering such a thing? And darn his hard-nosed, unmet-as-yet mother for reducing them both to this level. She looked down. Her bare toes wriggled back up at her. Shoes were suddenly symbolic of every struggle she'd ever faced with her parents or within herself. And Jay was still pacing around her kitchen. Obviously he didn't have a clue as to *why* he thought it important for her to make a good impression. "Oh, to heck with it," she snorted and slapped open the back door, refusing to consider shoes or even her flip-flops.

Catherine stopped so suddenly, Jay barely avoided colliding with her. She shifted back and forth on her feet in reaction to the sunburnt porch boards as she looked back over one shoulder at him. Darn it, some things could not be left to ride. Not if she was to have any self-respect at the end of this fiasco. Jay was using her family to impress his mother. That wasn't very nice. Her feet continued to shift as an awful thought bubbled its way up to her consciousness. What about her? Was she, on some subconscious level, falling for Jay because it would put her back in her parents good graces? Make up in some strange way for what her parents probably perceived as a slap to their exalted genetic code? Good grief, what a thought. "I am me," she told herself—and Jay—firmly. She wouldn't use him to impress her family, and by God, he wouldn't use her, either. She crossed her arms stubbornly and said, "I'm happy just the way I am, and I'm *not* going to change. I won't put on lipstick or shoes, but I won't ask you to take yours off, either. I'm afraid that's the best deal I can cut.''

Jay appeared to be having difficulty following the direction of her thoughts. ''Rosie, men don't wear lipstick.''

''Shoes, Jay. I was referring to keeping your shoes on.''

''Thank you. I will.'' He still looked confused.

''Why should I try to change myself to impress people? Why should you? We strike sparks off each other just the way we are. I refuse to trade on what was a simple accident of birth. Repeating my parents name like a mantra in front of your mother won't change anything. It'll probably just make her more disappointed when she finally sees me. If you're looking for a beautiful packaged IQ, then Susan's your ticket.'' She couldn't help sneaking in, ''It just seems to me, though, that if there was anything there, you'd have noticed by now. For crying out loud, you two work together on top of a major fault line in the earth's crust. Surely you'd have felt *something* shake by this time. Now, let's go in, my feet are frying on this hot porch floor.''

Jay blinked and stared at her momentarily. Then he took her hand, tucked it under his own, and said, ''It's time you met my mother. If you stand up to her half as well as you do to me, there won't be any problem.'' *He* couldn't keep himself from adding, ''Of course, if you'd worn some shoes, your feet wouldn't be affected by the hot floorboards.'' He turned quickly and purposely ushered her inside Iris's back door before she could think of a clever comeback.

So many innuendos from so many sources about dear, sweet Mama. Catherine was fairly sure she didn't want to meet the woman at all, at this point. If Iris couldn't live up to Mama's expectations, Catherine saw her own chances as slim. Of course, Catherine's living room wasn't decorated in egg-yolk yellow. Perhaps that would help.

Jay cleared his throat as he steered her through the kitchen. "We'll have to do this quickly," he warned. "I have to spend some time with Susan before dinner. I don't like the looks of the p waves in that batch of Mexican data she brought with her."

Catherine didn't like the look of the p waves right there in Iris's apartment. She was under the distinct impression she was about to go through a quake of her own in very short order. He wouldn't leave her to face his mother all alone, would he?

"It's possible it could be a bad quake, you know. The longer it takes for the p waves to come back up to normal from the original deviation, the worse the quake can be. Might even have to evacuate the area."

The waves vibrating around Catherine just then were having a bit of trouble coming back to center themselves—just in case he hadn't noticed. "Jay—" How could she delicately put that she'd personally feed him to his own seismograph if he so much as put a toe outside the front door before things were settled here?

"We'll just tell her that I'll help move her things when I get back and that I'll take care of getting something for dinner tonight. I'm bringing Susan over. Mother doesn't cook and Hollis and I are hopeless, so I'll bring something home with me."

The lovely Susan wasn't to cook? Maybe she couldn't. What a shame. "I'd be happy to make dinner for everyone," she offered magnanimously, willing to show off her own expertise.

But he brushed the offer off. "No, no. That's all right. It's Iris's first day home from the hospital. I don't think the extra confusion would be good for her." They were out of the kitchen and steaming through the dining room, on a collision course with the unhappy-looking group in the living room. "No, don't worry about it. Susan and I will find some catering place or a delicatessen that can help us out on the spur of the moment. Yes," he nodded. "That would be best."

How come Susan wouldn't add to the confusion while Catherine would? If he was thinking of the confusion of the last few days, that had been mostly the company she'd been keeping. Three little kids would add a certain helter-skelter touch to anyone's day. Brother, she'd give him a p wave he wouldn't soon forget. And the epicenter would be right between his two beautiful eyes.

Chapter Ten

Iris lay on her overstuffed floral sofa during the introductions. She looked very washed out and pale in contrast to the yolk-colored walls and vivid sofa cushions. "Catherine Rose Escabito, I'd like you to meet my mother-in-law, Carlotta Gand. Mother Gand, my next-door neighbor you've heard so much about, Catherine Rose."

Catherine took the opportunity presented as she and the older woman crossed the room toward each other to study the perfectly postured petite woman. Elegantly coiffed blue-rinsed white hair bouffanted around the patrician-featured face. The nubby-textured cinnamon suit on her slim, trim little body matched her expertly applied lipstick and nail polish exactly. She seemed very reserved, correct, proper, and Catherine felt a chill down her back at the prospect of sharing her apartment with such a paragon. Even during the heat of the summer day when anyone else would be sweltering in a suit, her hand was cool in Catherine's.

"How do you do, Miss Escabito." It was stated perfunctorily, as though she could not care less how she did.

"Please call me Catherine," she murmured politely.

There was no reciprocal offer.

"It's a pleasure to meet you, Mrs. Gand. I've heard a great deal about you, as well." Iris rolled her eyes behind the cinnamon-clad squared-back shoulders and Catherine tried not to laugh or choke on her words. Catherine knew from several of her friends's experiences that when one married, one didn't marry just a man, but rather a family. Resentful mothers could add a lot of stress to a marriage when they put their mind to it. Carlotta probably wouldn't even have to put her mind to it; it would just come naturally to her.

Catherine's gaze faltered a little at the cool direct gaze that met hers. It was the same color as Jay's, but there was none of the warmth of Jay's, none of the life. She looked to Iris for help, but Iris merely shrugged her shoulders impotently. Catherine's eyes swung back to Mrs. Gand and she tried to unstick her tongue from the roof of her mouth. "Mrs. Gand," she said, only to stumble to a halt when she was corrected.

"That's *Ms*. Gand."

"Sorry, *Ms*. Gand, I, uh, I just stopped by... to..." She couldn't make herself say it. Jay's mother raised one perfectly tweezed silver eyebrow at Catherine and calmly withdrew her hand from Catherine's clammy grasp. Catherine flushed and prayed Ms. Gand would not turn around in time to see the look of unholy amusement on Iris's face. Hollis squatted nearby, talking to little Tod, seemingly oblivious to the tension in the room. He'd grown up with her, Catherine reasoned. He probably was able to tune her out at will.

Catherine wiped her sweaty palm on the side of her shorts. Backing up, she tried to make a more coherent presentation. How hard could it be to offer somebody a bed for a couple of nights? Depended on the somebody. She was finding this to be extremely difficult. "Ms. Gand," she said more firmly. "What I'm trying to say—" if Iris didn't stop looking like she found Catherine's predicament so funny, she would leave without offering the invitation. She doubted her smile would last long after that "—is that I know how crowded the apartment must be for all of you, and the children do get up terribly early—"

"This morning's six o'clock was late for them." Iris interjected a little too eagerly, Catherine thought.

Ms. Gand made no comment, merely waited for Catherine to continue. Catherine worried that the woman might think Iris was trying to get rid of her, which of course, was exactly what Iris was trying to do.

"I'm sure you want to be close to your sons so that you can have a good visit. I just want you to know that if you find things are a little too cramped here, you're more than welcome to sleep in my spare bedroom. That way, you'd be just a hop, skip, and a jump away."

"I'm sure you'd rather have my Juli," Ms. Gand said with the certitude only a mother can have of a son's irresistibility. "Or has he already turned you down?"

The urge to announce just who had turned down whom was almost overwhelming, but a sideways glance at Jay was enough to tell her he would be hurt by such a public disclosure. She decided to swallow her pride. Catherine had enough experience with that that it was doubtful she'd choke on it. "I haven't asked him to stay," she stated in scrupulous honesty. "And I'd enjoy having you," Catherine stated firmly. What was one more cross to bear this week? It would give Iris some peace while she recovered. Iris nearly fell off the sofa behind her when Catherine waved dismissively, "Jay would only try and talk me into doing his laundry while he went off to study his p and s waves, not to mention the tsunami I was just hearing about.''

"I'm sure I raised better mannered sons than that." The lady wore her hauteur the way Queen Elizabeth wore her crown. Carlotta Gand held her head high. Only her eyes moved as she looked down the length of her straight nose—right on down to Catherine's bare symbols of her own personhood. Then she stared as though unable to quite believe what was right there in front of her.

"I'm sure you did. It was just a joke, Ms. Gand," Catherine sighed. It was going to be a very *long* two days unless this lady developed a sense of humor in one heck of a hurry.

"Presumably, the room won't be yellow, at least," the woman sniped, and Catherine could see the need to get her away from Iris before Iris burst open her stitches reaching to brain her.

"Uh, no. No yellow. Lot of blue, though. Blue's on the cool side of the spectrum, you know. You'll love it in this hot weather.'' And besides, it would match her personality to a T.

Ms. Gand sat down primly on the edge of a brown and yellow striped arm chair, the "companion" piece for the bright floral sofa. She looked expectantly first at Hollis and then Jay. When it became painfully obvious that no one was going to jump in protesting, "Oh, no, Mom, please don't go. We love you so. You must stay with us, here," she became even more prickly. "Well, that's just fine. I travel thousands of miles to be with my son in his hour of need and I get pushed off on a perfect stranger. That's gratitude for you. Well, someday in the not too far distant future, when I'm dead and gone, you'll all miss me.''

Somehow Catherine doubted that. Would one miss a migraine? She did suspect, however, that these motherly guilt-laying trips had been honed and polished through the years. But they'd evidently lost their effectiveness—probably from sheer overuse—for Hollis looked like he'd heard it all before and Carlotta seemed ready to slip off the chair's edge where she perched so perfectly when Jay chose to use the homily as an opportunity to tease Catherine instead of cowtowing to his mother.

"Oh, she's not a *perfect* stranger, Mom. She'll tell you herself, she has no real area of genius, just broad patches of competence. Rosie's only a slightly better than average stranger." He looked very pleased with his gentle ribbing.

Catherine laughed out loud.

Carlotta Gand turned red.

Iris held her stitches while she gave a slightly choked-sounding cough.

Hollis simply got up and carried his mother's baggage over, giving Catherine's arm a squeeze of gratitude as he did.

Catherine helped Carlotta Gand get settled. But the woman was so prickly, Catherine wanted nothing more than to go in and throw herself on the store's mercy. Surely all would be forgiven and she'd be allowed to work full days with maybe even some overtime if she explained her present circumstances. That would leave Carlotta to hurl her little barbs in an empty room. Catherine could feel herself starting to unravel around the edges. She was doing her best to keep from completely unwinding, but Carlotta kept picking at her seams with unerring accuracy.

"Here's the bathroom, right at the end of the hall."

"My God, it's more antiquated than next door."

Catherine pretended to misunderstand. "Yes, it is rather quaint, isn't it?"

Carlotta rolled her eyes. "Why does your mirror have *hematogenous* printed on it?"

Catherine took a glance. "Oh, that's a mistake." She tore the card down and taped up *cacography*. "*Hematogenous* was left over from yesterday," she said, as though that explained everything. She led the way out of the room, hoping Carlotta would let it drop. The other woman would probably consider her self-improvement attempts pathetic and more than likely pointless. "Towels are here. They're new so they should feel good."

Carlotta gave her an odd look and ran an experimental hand over one of the towels neatly stacked in the small hall linen closet. "Feels like a Brillo pad."

Catherine thought fast. "Well, they'll pinken your skin, remove all the dead cells. Think of it as an inexpensive pumice stone. And here's my bedroom."

"It should have flowers, mmm...there—on the end of the dresser."

"Yes, I ordered a silk arrangement the other day." Oh, God. They agreed on something. What kind of sign was that?

On it went. The bedspread in the guest room was the wrong tone of blue for the wall color. The dining room table was outsized for the room. Catherine's bare feet came back under scrutiny. Her toenails needed a pedicure. It was a losing war, and if crying "uncle" would have done any good, Catherine would have done so. Her inferiority complex hadn't had a field day like this since she'd moved out of her parents home several years back.

All she could think of was baking. It was that or shoot herself.

"It's too hot to be doing this, you know." Carlotta offered the criticism a little tentatively, as though beginning to have doubts about Catherine's ability to stay in touch with the real world.

"You're probably right."

"So why are we doing it?"

"I'm out of Twinkies."

"Am I supposed to understand that?"

Catherine had just about decided that the person didn't exist who could understand her. "No, probably not. Jay doesn't understand it, either."

"Oh, well as long as I'm not the only one."

"No, you're not." Catherine stood over the stove stirring Cheerios into butterscotch chips melted with peanut butter while Carlotta spooned teaspoonfuls of cookie dough onto a baking sheet. "I gave Jay the last of my marshmallows the other day," Catherine explained. "Or we could make Rice Krispie candy, too." And he was probably sharing the last bit of it with Susan right then, the rat. Her candy. Given to Susan. She needed to meet the guy who had coined the term "love/hate relationship." They were probably soulmates.

"This is revolting," Carlotta declared and shook her head in exasperation when Catherine's response was a simple, "Mmm."

"We're both going to be sick."

"Not me—I'm never sick." At least not physically. Her soul was a little ill at the moment. "I ate, what was it? I think eight...yes, eight packages of Twinkies just the other day. Jay got sick watching me, but I was fine."

Poor Carlotta had evidently gone into shock. Her comeback was nothing snappier then, "Merciful heavens."

"Not this week, they're not." They certainly weren't. Carlotta Gand had succeeded in resurrecting all her childhood insecurities. She'd convinced Catherine that sexy, warm, wonderful Jay would have to be given up. Like candy during Lent. It was the noble thing for her to do—he deserved an intellectual partner, an equal—but it hurt like hell.

Had he gotten the sex manual out of the library yet? Would his eye wink endearingly when he first focused on the pictures? Who would be sitting next to him when his eye kicked in? Oh God, she needed a Twinkie. Wait, she was out of those. That's why they were baking. Oh, oh, yes. She blinked herself back to reality. "Carlotta, I think that last batch of cookies might be done."

Carlotta opened the oven door, releasing another blast of hot air into the already furnacelike kitchen. "You're right. They are." She reached in with her hot pad and removed the perfectly browned cookies before popping in the next batch. She picked up a cookie, burning her fingers and fanning her mouth as she bit into the hot treat. "I can't not eat desserts. That's why I never make them. If they're in the house, I eat them."

My goodness. A crack in the façade. Didn't that just beat all? Catherine inspected the arrangement of chocolate chips in the cookie she was blowing on. "You should go running while you're here," she declared. "You won't gain an ounce that way. That's what I do. Poor Jay is convinced you have to be the best at whatever you do. But I only run so I can eat more. He sees it as some kind of fatal character flaw, I'm afraid."

"I always taught my boys to strive for the highest goals," Carlotta said, sounding proud. "For the life of me, though, I just can't figure what went wrong with Hollis."

"Hollis is as happy as an oyster. His wife and children are as precious to him as if they were pearls he formed himself in the oyster bed. Isn't that kind of happiness all a parent really wants for a kid?" Catherine asked rhetorically, effectively cutting off the woman yet again. "Now, we still have some of that good Belgian chocolate we chopped up for the cookies. I think I'll melt it down and make chocolate-dipped strawberries. Doesn't that sound good?"

"Iris has no taste."

"Big deal. She's a sweetheart. That's more important."

The look on Carlotta's face said she not only disagreed, but considered it pointless to argue with her. She moved right on. "Now Susan and Jay."

Uh-oh. Catherine just knew she didn't want to hear this.

"What a handsome couple they make! And with their collective IQ's, just think of the children they could produce."

Yes, just think. She got out the making for lemon bars, feeling her need for a sugar fix becoming more severe with Carlotta's every word.

"They have so much in common, working in the same field and all. Of course, she only has her masters, but I overheard her saying she was thinking about getting started on her Ph.D. I tell you, I get the shivers just thinking about how perfect a match like that would be."

What Catherine felt was more like a shudder. The kitchen suddenly felt chilly. "Things might not work out between the two of them," she offered weakly. "Jay doesn't seem to respond to her in that way..." *Oh, God, please don't let him respond to her that way.* Catherine knew she had to give him up herself, but please, not for dizzo Susan. He'd respected the other woman for nothing but her mind for the last two years, let him keep it up until his eyes were fully opened to the choices all around him.

But Carlotta sounded determined. "Well, I'll just have to give him a little guidance, that's all."

The only really human thing Catherine had noticed about Carlotta Gand so far was that she really did have a sweet tooth. She was eating yet another cookie as she continued, "She's perfect. Susan will never burden him with a pack of children. She has her own career to worry about. One or two would be all, I'd be willing to bet. And I'll be there to make sure he isn't distracted with a lot of silly things like Little League and school plays. I can attend those for him."

This lady had a desperate need to be needed! Was she so terrified of losing her children to adulthood? Unfortunately her misguided attempts to remain indispensable were alienating everybody—at least, Catherine thought they were. Brother, old Jay was in for one heck of a sterile existence. His mother seemed determined to keep him very narrowly focused and dependent upon her. Of course, he was a big boy now, all he had to do was speak up. But she couldn't keep quiet. "Jay may have other plans. It is his life," she said.

Carlotta waved that thought off. "Juli has always followed my suggestions. He knows I only have his best interest at heart."

Yeah, right.

The other woman had a cookie in each hand as she announced, "Well, I must go and freshen up if I'm to have dinner with them." She cast a critical eye over Catherine's flour-dusted shirtfront. "You, too," she commented.

She wondered if Johnny had learned how to put tacks on the chair of someone you disliked yet, or how to pull a chair out from under somebody just as they were about to sit on it. It wouldn't take long to teach such vital skills. No more than a few minutes with a child as quick as John. Was that what Ms. Gand had meant by making full use of your intellect?

Catherine brushed ineffectually at the flour on her shirtfront, making it worse as she added the layers from her hands. "Don't worry about me. I wasn't invited. It seems I'll add too much to the confusion level and put Iris back in the hospital." She remembered Jay's words with stinging clarity.

But it wasn't hard to see where Jay's lack of tact came from. Carlotta's mouth actually dropped open in surprise. "Well, of course you weren't invited. Juli needs to notice Susan—outside the office. And your presence in a room, well you're very *present* when you're in a room." She looked at Catherine critically. "I can't quite figure out why, but you take *over* a room." She shook her head. "No, I only meant you should clean up before you sit on any of the furniture or touch anything. What if someone stops by for a visit? They'll see you like that."

A fate worse than death, Catherine was sure. Keeping your shirtfront pristine in case someone dropped by was probably some kind of corollary to always wearing holeless underwear just in case you had an accident and had to go the hospital, she mused on the way to the bathroom and it was that final little criticism that did her in. Not losing the money, not Susan or Carlotta's arrival on the scene or Iris's brush with death. No, it was the sight of her floury clothing in the bathroom mirror that had her blubbering like a baby. She went and lay on her bed, curling into the fetal position while she tried to sort through the chaos in her mind and stop her tears.

She'd been foolish to think she had anything to offer Jay. Good grief, the man could hire a cook or a housekeeper. He had the money to pay for lessons if he ever decided he didn't like the atmosphere up in his ivory tower. Who did she think she was that she should insist on saving him from himself? *If* he decided he wanted saving, he was so darn smart he could take dancing lessons. French cuisine classes. Wines 101 and be suaver than suave in nothing flat.

He didn't need her. She didn't even have the intelligence to put an apron on and protect one of her favorite blouses. Ms. Gand wouldn't want someone like Catherine watering down the genes. She'd chew her up and not even bother to spit out the bones.

Catherine couldn't help loving Jay, but she could cut her losses. She did *not* need to stick around and watch the unfolding of Carlotta's grand plan. She was going to go visit somebody—her parents?—right after dinner and stay a few days. Carlotta could have her apartment all to herself and be welcome to it. But Catherine would go out in style with this dinner.

Catherine knew what she wanted for dessert. The chocolate-dipped strawberries would make her feel better, she was sure. So, for dinner, she wanted something a little elegant to complement them. She felt an inner need to prove herself, even though there would be no one around to impress with it. She made broccoli quiche. Sugar-burnt almonds and mandarin orange sections made the perfect foil for a fresh green salad made with three kinds of lettuce.

She was just about to sit down to a place setting of her good china and a linen napkin when the back door opened, allowing Iris to hobble in.

From her doubled-over posture, it was difficult to understand exactly what she was saying as her voice was aimed directly at the floor. "I've had surgery, for God's sake," she complained. "I need something basic for dinner. They're all in there eating caviar-topped, twice-baked potatoes. I can't stand caviar when I'm well!"

Catherine rose and set another place. She wasn't feeling particularly hospitable, but Iris *had* been ill. She instructed, "Sit down. Some of this quiche is just what the doctor ordered. Very basic. Eggs and cream. You'll love it."

Ten minutes later the back door swung open again, admitting one anxious husband. "Catherine Rose, is Iris—There you are! My God, I was worried. I thought you'd gone to the bathroom or something. Then when you never reappeared, I thought . . ." His eyes took in the laden table. "Wow, that looks good, especially those strawberries. Mind if I sit in for a minute? Lobsters and shrimp are best left out in the ocean, if you ask me. They remind me of trying to eat knuckles. We'll leave it to those highbrows across the way."

Catherine was still rummaging in the silverware drawer when a light tapping at the back door caused her head to swivel.

"May I come in?" Carlotta questioned through the screening.

"I guess," Catherine returned listlessly, holding the door for her even though there was nothing she'd rather do than tell the woman to take a hike. Susan should be warned as to what she was getting into. Catherine herself had decided to marry an orphan.

"The caterer Juli went to sent some absolutely awful dessert composed of mushy ladyfingers drenched in cherry liqueur. Dreadful. And the lobster was inedible, as well. Whoever put that poor thing to death was doing a great work of charity. It must have been the terror of the lobster beds. Tough as nails." The woman should have been Italian considering the elegant hand language that accompanied her words. Something had obviously upset her, for there was a real crack in her composure. "And that Susan! Why she doesn't listen to a word I say. I never realized how very *out of it* she is. For heaven's sake, she wants to quit her job when she starts her family, *and* she wants *six* children! Imagine expecting Juli to be the total support of that size family."

If only Catherine's head felt better, she would say something snappy about this proving there was a purpose for everything under God's heaven. Susan's was to frustrate Carlotta Gand and her grand scheme for Jay. Knowing Susan was out of Carlotta's graces enabled Catherine to give a wan smile as she directed, "Sit down and I'll get you a plate." The dinner party she'd been too gauche to attend seemed to be shifting course midmeal, she couldn't help but notice. If anybody else showed up, she'd have to get out the leaf for the table, and that was in storage down in the basement. Well, if anybody else showed up, they'd just have to go down and get it themselves. She was through being Ms. Nice Guy.

She threw up her hands when she turned to see Carlotta already seating herself. She'd lost all control of her life. She listened as Carlotta said, "Actually, I don't really need any main course. I was just wondering if there were any lemon bars left over from our bender this afternoon. Hello, Iris. Hollis. If you were trying to get away from me, you're out of luck."

"Now, Mom, it isn't what you're thinking," Iris hastily interjected. "We weren't trying to get away from you."

"That's good. I allowed myself to be shoved onto a perfect stranger to make everybody happy. I'll be darned if I'll go sit on the back stoop."

Carlotta had a sense of humor?

The woman settled into a chair and let Catherine put a plate and silverware in front of her. Even though she'd initially turned down the quiche, it must have gotten to her for she served herself a nice-sized wedge. "Well, there's not much point worrying about calories at this stage. I doubt I can count as high as I'd need to total up the day's intake. I'll diet when I get back home."

Catherine was too upset to be tactful any longer. Maybe she wasn't smart enough for Jay, but by God, he deserved better than a Susan. "You are aware, aren't you, Ms. Gand, that if Jay *was* to marry someone like Susan they'd likely pass out from the rarefied atmosphere in which they'd live?"

"What *are* you talking about?" Carlotta looked at her with all the disdain a pseudo-intellectual snob could muster. "California is absolutely beautiful. The smog problem is being dealt with."

"Oh, I'm not thinking of geographical location. I'm referring to the way they both have their heads up in the clouds all the time. Why Jay will have to recruit strangers in from off the streets to tell him what the problem is every time his children make a peep." She purposely made it sound like Jay was going to have piles of kids, just to annoy Carlotta.

Iris started sputtering and wheezing into her cup of Russian tea. Her eyes were watering, too. Catherine was too tired to tell if she was trying not to laugh or cry.

"You're jealous," Carlotta pronounced like an oracle from on high. She was in for a surprise if she expected Catherine to deny it.

"Maybe."

"I knew it! Any girl who sees my Juli wants him."

Spoken like a true mother.

"Juli needs somebody who has at least finished college." She said it as though personal worthwhileness was measurable by the number of degrees that hung from a belt like scalps. "Why, you'd have nothing in common at all."

"Actually I did."

"Did what?"

"Finish college."

"No!" It was long, drawn out, and full of disbelief.

Catherine merely shrugged. It hadn't been an Ivy League school. It had been the kind that was out scrabbling for students, not turning them away. But she *had* finished.

Across the table from her, Hollis looked pensive. He was tracing absent patterns on her linen tablecloth with his fingers when he spoke. "I don't know, Catherine Rose. Maybe he just needs time to get his priorities straightened out. After all, he's coming from years of tunnel vision and is only just now starting to develop peripheral sight and an itch to explore all the alleys and sideroads he's beginning to see."

Carlotta was an unbecoming shade of purple. It clashed with her cinnamon slacks and lip gloss. Catherine Rose played with the mist on her glass, letting the beads of moisture run down her fingertip as she watched Carlotta and thought out loud. "I'm not some orphan out begging for a home. It's funny, but I thought I was finally comfortable with who I am. Right now I feel about as appealing as the dented can bin where we toss reduced tin goods and they *still* don't sell. I just couldn't take getting involved with some guy who's going to spend our life together apologizing for me. Maybe Jay's roadmap to love and happiness requires a Ph.D. to read it. But if that's the case, I guess I need to just sit tight and wait for somebody with a less complicated rules-of-the-road guide—if there even is somebody out there with the simplistic one I evidently require."

"Oh, now, Catherine—"

"Eat your quiche, Hollis," his mother directed. "And mind your own business. I'm quite sure someone more Catherine's...ilk will turn up. She's absolutely right. She and Juli are simply too dissimilar for things to work between them."

That was probably fact, but she sure would have liked the opportunity to give it a shot. Catherine pasted a sickly smile on her lips—she absolutely would not cry in front of them—and agreed with at least part of Carlotta's thoughts. "Yes, let's finish eating while it's still warm." She did her best to keep the conversation light through the rest of the meal. She didn't want Iris or Hollis feeling sorry for her. She was a survivor—she'd make it. She didn't know what shape she'd be in, but she'd make it.

There was only one chocolate-covered strawberry and a handful of lemon bars left when Susan came through the back door. Everyone at the table stiffened—even Carlotta. Catherine truly hoped that Carlotta fully realized what a disaster a match between Susan and Jay would be. They would not complement or balance each other's weaknesses. Instead they would only reinforce each other's idiosyncrasies.

Susan's sunny bubbliness was looking a bit strained as she spoke. "I wanted to say good-bye to you all. As soon as I can find my car keys I'm going back to the hotel. I'll be flying out first thing in the morning." She looked so sad and lost, Catherine couldn't help but feel a little sorry for her. "I just wanted to say thank you for giving me some time alone with Jay." They all looked guiltily at each other. Lord, the woman was so out of it she hadn't even figured out everyone's leaving had been incredibly rude. Susan looked at Catherine and shrugged her shoulders helplessly, obviously at a loss as to how to gain Jay's attention. "He just keeps talking about *you*. The whole time I've been here, it's been Rosie this, and Rosie that. Rosie doesn't have any children, but Rosie knew immediately that he wanted his blanket. You should have seen Rosie handle the short-change artist while sweeping the floor and running the office with both hands tied behind her back."

Catherine's heart lurched a bit in her chest. Jay had sung her praises? Catherine popped the last strawberry into her mouth to keep herself from consoling Susan on her lack of success. She had a cousin who was bright *and* had both feet on the ground. He'd be a perfect match for Susan, but Jay wasn't the one for the other woman. Not her Jay.

"Well, maybe back in California... Who knows?" Susan made a helpless little gesture with her hands and left. The door slammed shut behind her.

"Don't worry, Catherine Rose," Hollis quickly interjected as Catherine stared at the closed door. "If she hasn't made any progress in the last two years, it's unlikely anything will happen in the next few weeks."

Catherine stood. Her nerves were just about shot. She would have to be a saint to not feel totally stressed out by this juncture, and as far as she knew, no one had put her name in for canonization. She was just about to say something along those lines when the phone rang. She answered on the kitchen extension, and the threesome at the table could hear everything.

"Hello? Oh, I've been keeping busy." Now there was a classic understatement. "What's up? No, wait. Let me guess. They found a tunnel under the safe. Some mole took the money. Well, it makes as much sense as anything else I've thought of so far. Are they asking for a lie detector test yet? I didn't have time to conduct an extensive physical search. I had just finished going over the figures when they threw me out of the place. But if it was just laying around on the floor somewhere, surely I would have noticed. Tripped over it, or something.... You're kidding! They found it? Where? Good grief, I never would have thought of looking there."

Carlotta, Iris, and Hollis watched as Catherine shook her head in disbelief. "Unbelievable. It must have slipped down when I was in a hurry to lock up the night before and I didn't notice. Who found it? Tell Gary I'm his slave forever. It was between the safe and its protective wooden box. I can't believe it. Yeah, thanks. I appreciate that you kept trying to reach me. It's a real load off my mind. 'Bye."

Catherine wore a genuine smile when she came back to the table. At least she'd have a way of paying the rent and if she worked long enough and hard enough, she just might forget all that might have been with Jay. "That was a friend of mine from the number seven store. They brought her in to replace me when I was outlawed from the place. Guess what?''

"Rosie? Could I speak to you alone for a minute, please?" It was Jay. He had come in silently behind her.

She ought to seriously consider replacing her back screen door with one of those automatic opening pneumatic ones like they had at the store. It would save wear and tear on the arm muscles of the entering and exiting throngs. "This is a pretty small apartment, Jay. There really isn't anyplace terribly private to go." Okay, so she was noble enough to give up her dreams and had admitted Jay needed more than she could ever give him. That did not mean she had to be martyr of the year and sequester herself off with him so he could rub her face in what she'd be missing.

Jay looked around at the assembled group. He tried giving them all meaningful looks, but they didn't seem to get the hint. He finally put it into a direct request. "Could I be alone with Rosie for a moment, please?"

"My side hurts too much to move right now."

"I have to stay and make sure Iris doesn't faint or anything. Her side hurts."

"And I want to make sure you don't do anything foolish that will affect your entire future."

Jay scowled at the lot of them. Turning to Catherine, he baldly announced, "I asked Susan what she thought the chances of you and me making it together might be. I thought it might be good to get a woman's perspective."

Good grief. The blind leading the blind.

"She said we're too different, that we'd be an intellectual Mutt and Jeff team."

. The fact that Susan was probably right did not assuage the pain Catherine felt. In fact, if Susan hadn't already taken off, Catherine would have saved her the price of a ticket and sent her back to California herself—without benefit of the airplane. "Is that right?" Catherine sat back down and gazed up at him from the table. "What do you think, Jay?" She couldn't help it. She needed to know.

Jay studied the floor before looking up a little shyly at her. "I think I don't care what Susan thinks. She's just plain wrong. Naturally you'd have to help me a bit, show me how to run the washers and dryers of life. But I'm fairly intelligent. I can learn."

What? *What? Jay* was feeling inferior? This was too much. "Jay, what are you saying?"

A look of sheer panic marched across his mother's face. "He's just feeling guilty, can't you see that? You're a young woman, attractive, lost your job, no money to pay the rent, you've given him a hand once or twice in the past week . . . It's just sympathy. He doesn't know the money's been found."

Catherine almost wept. It would be like Jay to try to be noble. She couldn't hold him to it. Catherine forced herself to look at him. The expression on his face registered, even through the film forming over her eyes. He studied his mother like he would a seismograph readout that had been handed to him upside-down. It was something you thought you were familiar with, yet here it was looking totally foreign.

"That's the most asinine thing I've ever heard," he finally told his mother. His eye hardly blinked at all. "I'd have to be a total idiot to marry for reasons like that."

"I've always protected you from life's harsher realities, Juli. You might be taken in—"

"All that protecting was a real disservice, Mom. There's nothing cute about an incompetent adult."

Catherine sat in her chair chewing her lip. She stared up at Jay, unable to believe the newfound strength of purpose his face fairly radiated. He was a wonder.

"I've learned how to run a load through the washer and I've even figured out not to put jeans in with my white underwear. I can just as easily learn to use a lawnmower and hang pictures on the wall for Rosie. I can do these things. I will do them. I'll learn how to make Rosie happy."

"But Jay," Catherine said. "My IQ is only one hundred and fifteen. You'll be bored with me."

Jay looked positively fierce. "Don't insult yourself or me. There is no way you will ever bore me. The converse is much more likely."

She get bored with him? Catherine found the concept entirely ludicrous. Never.

Carlotta stood, leaving one hand clenched on the tabletop. "I worked hard to keep your time free for learning, so you could take advantage of your gifts."

"You left me a cripple unable to operate anywhere but the work arena."

Slowly, Carlotta Gand's face crumbled. "You don't appreciate me. I'm leaving first thing in the morning."

"That's your prerogative," Jay responded in a slightly more gentle tone. "But I'd like you to stay. I'd like you to get to know Catherine . . . and me. Please stay."

"Yes, stay," Catherine reiterated. She could put up with anything if Jay was part of the deal.

"I've thought about this a lot, Mom," Jay assured her. "Susan's being here reminded me of how sterile my life back in California really is. Rosie introduced me to color and laughter, love and joy. I need her, Mom. I want you here when we marry. If she says yes, that is." He looked at Catherine, his face shyly questioning.

She wanted to say yes so badly her eyes practically crossed from the effort of holding her agreement back. "Are you *sure*, Jay? You want me just as I am? You're not going to apologize for me or try to change me?" She needed to know he would be content with what he got.

"Rosie, anybody not happy with you would have to be certifiably crazy," he assured her gallantly. "I admit I tottered on the brink of insanity for a while, but I'll thank God every day from this point on that I came to my senses in time. That is if you'll have me." He looked at her pleadingly. "Please have me, Rosie."

"Oh, I'll have you." Her smiled blossomed, transforming her slightly better-than-average face into true beauty. "Just the way you are, blinking eye and all—I'll have you every day for the rest of our lives. It feels like I've loved you forever, Jay."

His mother lifted her head from her hands and sounded surprised. "Why, Juli, I didn't know you were capable of such intense feelings. You never seemed interested in anything but your books before."

"It was beautiful, wasn't it?" Iris contributed, wiping a tear from her eye. "All I got was a diamond in a plastic Easter egg."

Hollis looked insulted as he picked up his wife and prepared to carry her back to their apartment. "It was very good chocolate and a very good diamond in that Easter basket, you ingrate," he groused as he carried her out the door.

Carlotta followed them, her mind already whirring along new lines. "You should carry roses, Catherine," she said, "for your middle name. We'll make the bouquet multi-hued, since Jay says you brought color into his life." She stopped in her tracks. "Is that all right with you?"

"It's fine." Catherine's smile was radiant. Carlotta Gand's roses were fine. Life was fine. Jay was finer than fine.

Then the room was suddenly empty of all audiences. Jay took her hands in his, his eyes never losing contact with hers. "Would you mind living in California, or shall I look for something here?"

She laughed. "What would an earthquake specialist do in Chicago?"

"Oh, honey, don't you know? As long as we're together, we'll create our own temblors."

He leaned down and gently placed his lips over hers and Catherine swore the earth moved beneath her feet.

* * * * *

Silhouette Romance®

COMING NEXT MONTH

#730 BORROWED BABY—Marie Ferrarella
A Diamond Jubilee Book!
Stuck with a six-month-old bundle of joy, reserved policeman Griff Foster
became a petrified parent. Then bubbly Liz MacDougall taught him a
thing or two about diapers, teething, lullabies and love.

#731 FULL BLOOM—Karen Leabo
When free-spirited Hilary McShane returned early from her vacation,
she hadn't expected to find methodical Matthew Burke as a substitute
house-sitter. Their life-styles and attitudes clashed, but their love
kept growing....

#732 THAT MAN NEXT DOOR—Judith Bowen
New dairy owner Caitlin Forrest was entranced by friendly neighbor Ben
Wade. When she discovered that he wanted her farm, however, she
wondered exactly how much business he was mixing with pleasure.

#733 HOME FIRES BURNING BRIGHT—Laurie Paige
Book II of HOMEWARD BOUND DUO
Carson McCumber felt he had nothing to offer a woman—especially
privileged Tess Garrick. Out to prove the rugged rancher wrong, Tess was
determined to keep all the home fires burning....

#734 BETTER TO HAVE LOVED—Linda Varner
Convinced she'd lose, loner Allison Kendall had vowed never to play the
game of love. But martial-arts enthusiast Meade Duran was an expert at
tearing down all kinds of defenses.

#735 VENUS de MOLLY—Peggy Webb
Cool, controlled banker Samuel Adams became hot under the collar when
he thought about his mother marrying Molly Rakestraw's father. But that
was before he met the irrepressible Molly!

AVAILABLE THIS MONTH:

Silhouette Romance®

A duo by Laurie Paige

There's no place like home—and Laurie Paige's delightful duo captures that heartwarming feeling in two special stories set in Arizona ranchland. Share the poignant homecomings of two lovely heroines—half sisters Lainie and Tess—as they travel on the road to romance with their rugged, handsome heroes.

A SEASON FOR HOMECOMING—Lainie and Dev's story...available now.

HOME FIRES BURNING BRIGHT—Tess and Carson's story...coming in July.

Come home to A SEASON FOR HOMECOMING (#727) and HOME FIRES BURNING BRIGHT (#733)...only from Silhouette Romance!

Take 4 bestselling love stories FREE
Plus get a FREE surprise gift!

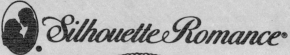